Shadow Acres

Shadow Acres

Frances Y. McHugh

Thorndike Press • Chivers Press
Thorndike, Maine USA   Bath, England

This Large Print edition is published by Thorndike Press, USA and by Chivers Press, England.

Published in 2001 in the U.S. by arrangement with Maureen Moran Agency.

Published in 2001 in the U.K. by arrangement with the author.

U.S. Hardcover 0-7862-3138-6 (Candlelight Series Edition)
U.K. Hardcover 0-7540-4432-7 (Chivers Large Print)

The text of this Large Print edition is unabridged.
Other aspects of the book may vary from the original edition.

Set in 16 pt. Plantin by Elena Picard.

Printed in the United States on permanent paper.

British Library Cataloguing-in-Publication Data available

Library of Congress Cataloging-in-Publication Data

McHugh, Frances Y.
    Shadow acres : a novel / by Frances Y. McHugh
    p. cm.
    ISBN 0-7862-3138-6 (lg. print : hc : alk. paper)
    1. Large type books. I. Title.
PS3563.C3685 S53 2001
813′.54—dc21   00-053631

Shadow Acres

Chapter One

Just as all roads used to be said to lead to Rome so, perhaps, all roads of my life have led to Shadow Acres.

Hindsight is always better than foresight, but we do not get a chance to use it. All we have to go on is what foresight we are capable of at the time.

Looking back on that fateful week I spent at Shadow Acres in December of 1966, I can't help but wonder if I was responsible for what happened. *If* I hadn't broken my engagement to Greg two years ago, *if* I hadn't become engaged to his cousin Bryan six months ago, *if* I'd never become involved with the Sedgwick family at all — would all of the terrible things that happened — or the ones that almost happened — ever have been triggered?

But can we control our destiny? One thing is certain; we can't control our birth into the family to which we are born. Nor can we control the destiny of that family, or of the families or people who touch their lives. Therefore I can't help wondering *if* I had

7

never existed — would the tragedies have happened at Shadow Acres?

Perhaps it all began the day I was born, December 22nd, 1945. I was almost a Christmas baby — but not quite — as I was almost a Christmas bride in the year 1966. Anyway, one thing I am sure of is that on the day I was born I didn't know what was going to happen at Shadow Acres during the week before Christmas 1966. Nor did anyone who welcomed me into the world.

The question in my mind is — did it all begin the day I was born? Or did it just begin Wednesday evening, December 14, 1966 — a week and a day before I was going to marry Bryan Sedgwick?

Perhaps I should have taken heed of the premonition I had on that Wednesday evening. It began with the feeling that time was a horrible, carnivorous monster and would soon catch up with and devour me. It hovered over me like a beast of prey as I sat at the mahogany baby grand piano in my three-room apartment on East Eighty-First Street and practised over and over a passage in Chopin's *Fantaisie Impromptu* in C# minor which I was to play at the music school Christmas recital the following Wednesday evening. The *Fantaisie Impromptu* is always popular because it was from the *Moderato Cantabile* portion of it that "I'm Always Chasing Rainbows" was virtually swiped, which gives even people who are not musically inclined a feeling of identification with it.

Outside on East Eighty-First Street, it was blowy, cold and sleety. Soon Bryan Sedgwick, my fiancé, would come, and I would have to stop my practising and give him my undivided attention.

The door chime sounded sooner than I expected, and I hurried to the door. Opening it, I stepped aside to let in a cold, wet and disgruntled Bryan. He frowned as he asked, "Still practising?" Then he took off his wet coat, hung it on a hanger in the small hall closet and strode into the living room. He never wore a hat on his well shaped head, and his straight, closely cut blond hair glistened with moisture.

He walked over to the piano and closed it with a bang, and I followed him, watching unhappily. When the lid covered the black and white keys, I said, "You know you can't shut off my music as easily as that."

He turned to look at me, his dark blue eyes troubled, his broad shoulders beneath his dark blue business suit squared. "Ready to go?" he asked, ignoring my remark. I noticed his shirt was white, his knit tie a blue that was close to the color of his eyes. "Go? Where?" I asked.

"I thought we'd have dinner at Marietta's, then see that new foreign movie at The Paris."

I sighed. "Oh, must we? I'd planned on having dinner here. I have a casserole in the oven and a nice big bowl of salad chilling in the refrigerator."

He sat down on the piano bench and took a cigarette case from his coat pocket, selected a cigarette and lit it. After he'd blown smoke up to the ceiling, he said, "Eat it for lunch tomorrow. What's the use of staying here and being bored to death? It's gloomy enough outside tonight."

I clasped my hands in front of me. They were suddenly cold. "That's a good reason for staying in." I glanced around my large dropped living room. Lamps were placed in strategic places beside easy chairs, and I had all the lamps lit. The result was a bright, cheerful and invitingly comfortable room. "Besides, I'd like to get to bed early so I can get up early tomorrow. I have a lot of practising to do, and tomorrow we have the Danas' dinner dance. I'll have to take time out in the afternoon to have my hair done for that. It will be a late night. And Friday I have a fitting for my wedding dress."

He sighed and looked down at his cigarette. "Reda," he said, "you and I have got to have an understanding!"

"About what?"

"About this constant practising of yours." He looked at me, and his eyes darkened. His nicely shaped lips were drawn tightly over his even white teeth, and he was crushing his cigarette in strong tense fingers.

I sat down in a nearby chair, feeling suddenly weak in the knees. "But we had that all out when we were first engaged. You said then you didn't mind my going on with my music after we were married."

"Well, I do. I've changed my mind. I don't want a life like Uncle Gregory had with Natalie."

"What have they got to do with it?"

"Everything. I'm not going to be made a fool of, like Uncle Gregory was."

"Nobody made a fool of your Uncle Gregory. And he and Natalie were very happy. At least they would have been if the family had let them alone."

"That's all *you* know about it. Aunt Natalie had men by the dozens."

I sat up straight and gripped the arms of the chair. "That's not true! And you know it! And besides, Natalie and I are very different. She was on the stage, and I'm going

11

to do concert work — if I'm good enough."

"Same difference. You'll be on a stage, for everyone to stare at, just like she was."

I jumped up. "Oh, that's ridiculous! If you don't like it, perhaps we'd better not get married!"

He stood up then, slowly, and very deliberately darkened his cigarette in a large cut glass ash tray I kept on a table especially for him. Then he came over and took me in his arms. "You don't mean that," he said, his face rubbing gently against mine. "You couldn't do without me. Could you?" he teased. Or was he teasing? Did he really think I couldn't do without him? His lips began to slide around to mine, and I felt mine, of their own volition, turning to meet them. "I wouldn't want to have to," I admitted, just before our lips met. His arms tightened around me, and my body thrilled at his closeness. A week from tomorrow we were going to be married. Then I would have his arms and lips for always.

I closed my eyes and gave myself up to the moment, not wanting it to end, afraid for it to end. When he was holding me close like that, I forgot everything — the world and everyone in it. Or almost everyone.

Several minutes later, when we were both breathless and trembling, he stopped kissing me, gently putting me away from him. Then he smiled in a way that always made him look like a small boy who had been in the cookie jar but knew he wasn't going to get scolded. "And that, my dear young lady, is the reason you'd better get your wrap and come to Marietta's for dinner. You are not safe here, alone with me."

I had to laugh. "You don't scare me a bit," I said. "But I suppose there's no use arguing with you."

That was the way it always ended. Bryan always got his way.

Later, as we were having spumoni and coffee at Marietta's, which was one of the better Italian restaurants down on Third Avenue in the Fifties, he reached for my left hand and began fingering my diamond engagement ring. It was a very beautiful, large stone, and had cost far more than Bryan should have spent. But when I scolded him, he had just smiled and said, "Stop complaining. Diamonds are a girl's best friend."

"Come to think of it," he said now, with a twinkle in his dark blue eyes, "maybe it would be a good idea for you to keep on with your music. If you make money with it, it will come in handy when I inherit Shadow Acres. That place costs a fortune to run, and

13

my income wouldn't begin to cover it."

I quickly pulled away my hand. "That's a strange thing to say. How do you know you will inherit Shadow Acres? Besides, Mr. Sedgwick is still hale and hearty. And he's only sixty-three."

He shrugged. "That doesn't mean he'll live forever. And I'll probably be his only heir."

"What about Greg? And Greg's father?"

"Oh, he disinherited them a long time ago. Uncle Gregory is always here, there and all over, covering some newspaper story, and doesn't see Granddad very often. And I don't believe anyone knows where Greg went after —"

"I don't believe Mr. Sedgwick would disinherit his son Gregory or his grandson Greg, even after what happened two years ago. Besides, if you were the only heir, you'd have more than enough to run Shadow Acres."

"Time will tell." He smiled as if he had a little private secret all to himself. It annoyed me. I said, "And besides, I wouldn't want to live at Shadow Acres. It —"

His eyes searched mine. "Has too many memories?"

I looked down into my coffee cup. "Maybe. I had some nice times there — before everything exploded."

His dark blue eyes darkened. They had a habit of darkening when he was serious about something. "Knowing what you mean, I don't like that remark, Reda," he said, his jaw tensing.

I crumpled my napkin and threw it on the table. "Let's go!" I said. "I'm tired. We've been out every evening for two weeks, and I'm exhausted. I want to go home."

"What about the movie?" he asked as he motioned to the waiter for the check.

"I don't want to see it. Please, Bryan, I'm so tired."

He shrugged. "Okay. We'll go home."

At the door to my apartment, he said, "If you're so tired, I won't come in."

I put my face up for his good night kiss. "Thanks, Bryan. I'll see you tomorrow. About six-thirty?"

He kissed me lightly but didn't take me in his arms. "Good night, Reda," he said, and let me unlock my door and walk into my apartment. Then he took the door-knob in his hand and closed the door between us before I could turn around and do it. I had the feeling he was glad to get away from me. Well, maybe I was a spoilsport, but I just couldn't keep on the go all the time the way he did.

It was only nine-thirty, but I went right to

bed, although I didn't go right to sleep in spite of my exhaustion. I felt let down, as if the bottom had dropped out of my stomach. Sometimes it was so nice to be with Bryan. When there were other people around, he was fun. But when we were alone, we never seemed to have much to say to one another. And often we argued, then made up, as we just had. I wondered if our entire married life was going to be like that.

Bryan Sedgwick was an ambitious young man, he was interested in banking. Only a year ago he had graduated from Yale, and already he had a good position with a New York bank, in the Loan Department, and rumor was that he would rise to better and better positions as the years went by if he kept up the good work.

His mother and father had been killed in a plane crash the year before he graduated from college. They had been returning from a vacation in Europe, and the plane ran into a storm and went down in the English Channel. All were lost.

It had hit Bryan hard, as he and his mother were very close. As to his father — he had a deep respect for him, but I don't believe they had ever been at all close. His father had been strict with him and had tried to counteract the overindulgence of his mother, but had not succeeded too well. As a consequence, Bryan had grown up to be rather spoiled and used to getting his own way.

His father had always made a good salary, and they had lived well. They had a large colonial house near ours in Greenwich, Connecticut, belonged to a country club, took nice trips in the summer and counted their friends among the so called "well to do."

It was therefore a surprise when it was learned that they had always lived up to and sometimes beyond their income. This meant that when his parents died so suddenly, Bryan was left with nothing but the heavily mortgaged house — and his good education.

His grandfather assisted him until he graduated, then helped him get his job in the New York bank. Then he told Bryan that from then on he was on his own. He believed in every man hoeing his own row, as he expressed it. Which was strange, considering the fact that he himself had fallen heir to his father's successful law practise.

Bryan hadn't liked the idea of being on his own quite so soon, but made up his mind he would make good — just to prove that he could. And he had. Going into the bank as a teller, at a very modest salary, he had quickly worked up to his present position by taking banking courses at night and applying himself with a dedication that surprised everyone.

Although I had not liked him too much as we were growing up, I had, in the last year, learned to love and respect him. However, sometimes I couldn't help wishing his mother hadn't indulged him quite so much. It still showed sometimes. And even though I understood the reason for it, I often found it irksome.

But after we were married, he would probably change. I would be patient with him and, loving him, I too would indulge him. But I'd also expect him to indulge me once in a while. And I was sure he would, because fairness was one of his good points. And if I went sixty percent of the way, I was sure he would come the other forty percent.

I remember my mother saying that marriage, to be a success, had to be ninety-ten on both sides. Well, I knew better than to expect it to be that way with Bryan, but I was confident I could work it out on the sixty-forty plan.

At last I fell asleep, and when I awoke, bright and early, I discovered I was nicely rested and would be able to spend the necessary long hours at the piano before going to the hairdresser's.

Chapter Two

That night I'd just finished dressing for the Danas' dinner dance when my phone rang. It was Mr. Sedgwick, Bryan's grandfather. He said, "I must see you immediately, Reda. Can you come up here at once?"

"But I'm all dressed for the Danas' dinner dance," I protested. "It's being given in honor of Bryan and me."

"I'm sorry, my dear," Mr. Sedgwick said. "But this is more important. You *must* come. And come alone!"

"What about Bryan? He'll be here for me in a few minutes!"

"Never mind Bryan!" Mr. Sedgwick snapped. "Come quickly! If you start now, you should be here about eight. And drive. Don't come by train. It would take too long." He sounded agitated, impatient, not at all like himself.

"Is there anything — ?" I was going to ask if there was anything wrong, but there was the click of the replaced receiver, and he was done. There was nothing I could do but obey. He had been too good a friend to me

19

not to heed his request, and I knew he would never send for me like that unless there was something seriously wrong.

I called the garage where I kept my car and had them bring it around, and while I waited I tried to get Bryan on the phone. But there was no answer. He was probably on his way up from his apartment down on East Thirty-Sixth Street. Well, it couldn't be helped. I dared not waste a minute. Mr. Sedgwick had sounded extremely upset, and I'd never known him to be that way before.

As I went out, I told the doorman to tell Bryan I'd had to go out, but that I'd get back as soon as I could and to make my apologies to the Danas. I would have to miss the dinner, but he should go on without me; I'd probably be able to get there in time for some of the dancing.

I entered the East River Drive as soon as I could and drove as fast as I dared in the early evening traffic, past the ghostly-looking ships in the river, through the arcades formed by the apartments and hospitals that were built out to the water's edge, skirting obstructions where repairs were always being made on the drive, through the Bronx and its tall, sterile-looking apartments with all the windows lighted, and onto the Thruway that would take me to Greenwich, where Shadow Acres was located.

I left the Thruway at the first Greenwich exit and drove to the rural road that led to Shadow Acres, being careful to make the turn where, about a mile from the house, a large elm tree took up half the road. It was a dangerous spot, and the county was always threatening to take down the tree and straighten the curve. But so far it hadn't been done.

It was a bad night for driving, misty and sleety, and I had to strain my eyes when I finally turned my car onto the long, narrow driveway that led from the road to the house of Shadow Acres. By that time, it was impossible to see through the impenetrable gray fog that had gradually closed in. But at last I drew up before the large bulk of the house. There were lights in the hall and in the library, which was to the right of the hall as you went in.

I left my car in the front driveway, gathered up the long, full skirt of my blue chiffon evening gown and ran quickly up the wooden porch steps of the old house.

The foghorns on the water in the distance were groaning their warning to all ships with a frightening persistence, and I shivered and wrapped my mink cape more closely about me.

The outside of the house of Shadow Acres always gave me the creeps, even in the sunshine, although the inside had a gracious, charming atmosphere, given to it by the late Mrs. Sedgwick who had passed away five years ago.

I glanced around nervously. Did I imagine that dark spot that loomed up in the fog at the corner of the house? I must have, because as suddenly as it had appeared, it disappeared.

I wanted to turn and run. But I was being silly, like a child afraid of the dark. I'd feel better when I was inside, with the door closed against the fog.

I rang the bell and could hear it peal through the large old house. Trembling slightly, I waited for the slow, deliberate footsteps of John, the butler. But there was no sound from within. No one came to admit me. I rang again, and the peal of the bell seemed to intensify the stillness. I lifted the knocker and let it drop with a resounding thud, and to my surprise, the heavy, handcarved, black walnut door swung open at my touch. I took a step forward and looked into the hall. It was empty. I stepped inside.

I'd always felt the old-fashioned staircase winding up to the balcony of the second floor stood there to welcome all guests. But tonight it seemed threatening. The grandfather clock nestling in the bend of the stairs ticked unusually loudly. Or was it because of the strange stillness of the house?

Again I had the desire to turn and run, to get back into my car and drive away from the place as quickly as the speed limit would permit me to.

But I conquered my panic. It must be nerves, I told myself. Too much pre-wedding excitement, and too many long hours practising at the piano for the concert at the music school, where I was studying.

I had known this house ever since I was born. There was no reason for me to feel frightened about visiting it.

I called, "Ooohooo! Mr. Sedgwick. Hello there. Where is everybody?" But my words echoed through the empty hall and seemed to rise and roll around the second floor balcony, then to rise still higher to the dome of stained glass that topped the rotunda of the large center hallway.

A cold chill slithered up my spine. "John!" I called a bit hysterically. Surely the butler or his wife, Agnes, must be around somewhere. But there was no sound other than the ticking of the grandfather clock.

Then I remembered — it was Thursday. John and Agnes were out. Mr. Sedgwick always let them go together, and on Thursdays had his dinner in town, at his club, before coming home. Apparently tonight he'd come straight home from the city. Probably Agnes had left something in the refrigerator for him.

I laughed a little with relief. Then the sound froze in my throat, for slowly, stealthily, the large oak door to the library where Mr. Sedgwick usually spent his evenings swung open. I gave a strangled cry, expecting I knew not what, but least of all what I saw!

"Bryan!" I gasped, for it was my fiancé and one of Mr. Sedgwick's two grandsons who had pushed open the door. He was in evening clothes, and he stood there looking at me. He had a revolver in his hand. His short blond hair was standing up almost straight. His handsome face was white. He seemed to be in a state of shock. His deep blue eyes were glazed and unseeing, like those of a blind man. Then slowly he seemed to recognize me.

"He's dead!" he said simply, as if he were saying, "It's eight o'clock," which the grandfather clock began to assure us it was by its whirring, twanging sounds.

I ran to the doorway, but he stopped me. "Don't go in," he said.

I looked past him and could see on the floor a pair of feet in the carefully polished black shoes Mr. Sedgwick always wore. They were sticking out from behind the desk in the center of the room, and they looked stiff and lifeless.

The French windows at the far side of the room were open slightly, and the curtains were moving back and forth from the current of air coming in from the garden.

I put a shaking hand up to my aching throat and stared at Bryan. He was still holding the gun.

"Why did you do it?" I cried. Then I ran to him and flung my arms about him, tears coursing down my cheeks. "Oh, why?" I cried frantically, holding him close, as if to protect him, or share with him whatever the future might hold for us both. I tried not to remember what he had said the previous evening about inheriting Shadow Acres. Had he known he would — so soon? Had he planned it that way?

His arms went around me, holding me in a desperate embrace for a moment. Then he pushed me from him. He seemed at last to have himself under control. "I didn't do it!"

he said thickly. "He phoned me to come here at eight — alone. When I got here, I came in with my key, as I always do, and found him dead with a bullet through his temple. I ran over to him and picked up the gun. And then you came. I didn't know what to do. I didn't know why you were here, and I didn't want you to know I was here. I thought if I kept still you'd go away." He dropped his hands down at his sides, his right hand still holding the gun. He looked very tired, as tired as I'd felt the night before. I sank down on a nearby chair. My knees would no longer hold me up. That always seemed to happen to me when I was emotionally upset.

I'd been fond of the elderly lawyer. He'd been my father's partner until Dad's death last year; since then he'd been sort of a guardian, handling my estate and keeping a fatherly eye on me as well as on Bryan.

As a matter of fact, my mother and father and I had been treated as part of the Sedgwick family as far back as I could remember. Mr. Sedgwick had treated my father as a son, my mother as a beloved daughter-in-law and me as a grandchild. All of which had been very nice for us, because we Randalls were without relatives of our own, my mother and father having been orphans when they met and married.

My memory of the elder Gregory Sedgwick was that he was a strong man in both mind and body. The entire Sedgwick family were good looking, and the men were all tall, handsome and well built, starting with Mr. Sedgwick, who was — had been — six feet, weighing about 180 pounds, with wavy dark brown hair which by now had turned gray, and large, intelligent brown eyes, like his son, who had been named after him, and his grandson, also named after him. Bryan took after his mother, who had blond hair and deep violet eyes.

The elder Gregory Sedgwick was a man who insisted on honesty and truth at all costs, and while he was kind to those he loved, he could be hard and ruthless to those who did not walk the straight and narrow. Yet he was not a prude, nor was he narrow-minded. He believed everyone should have a fair chance and as far as was in his power, he saw that everyone who came in contact with him got one.

I can remember how he used to play with us when we were kids — Bryan, Greg and me. When we were small he would let us climb all over him and pull his hair and search in his pockets for small surprises which he made a point of always having for us. Sometimes it was just a small toy, sometimes candy, sometimes just bright, shiny pennies. But there was always something.

When we began to grow up and played games around the house, he would insist we all play fair, never cheat, and whoever lost had to take it with a good grace. "You have to be a good sport," he used to tell us. "Nobody likes a poor loser."

I remembered his face so well. It was a large face, with a fan of small lines at the corners of his brown eyes from his ever ready smile, with a line running down each side of his mouth starting from his nose, which came, I used to think, from the way he would tighten his jaw when he was displeased.

He had large strong hands with small golden brown hairs on the backs of them that continued all the way up his muscular forearms. And when you got close to him, he always had a clean, mannish smell which was a combination of good pipe tobacco, soap and after shave lotion. He never smoked cigarettes.

When my mother died, he came to see us and comforted us, reminding us that we still had each other and the entire Sedgwick family. And when my father died, he came to the house and took complete charge.

When it was all over, he took me home to Shadow Acres and saw to it that Bryan kept me too busy to think. Greg wasn't there, and I'd never missed him so much.

It was he who advised me to sell the house and move into the city. And it was he who encouraged me to enroll in the music school.

When Greg and I split up, he sternly told me to be sure I was doing the right thing. "But how could I marry him after — ?" I cried. He gave me a long, piercing look. "That's up to you," he said. "I'm sure Greg wouldn't want you if you don't trust him."

When Bryan and I told him about our engagement, he said, "Just be sure. Especially you, Reda." I knew what he meant. He wanted me to be sure I had put Greg out of my heart. And I had, or thought I had.

He was a combination of strength, gentleness, wisdom, kindness, justice — and above all he was a man. A man to reckon with. A man to love. A man you could depend on. A man you could trust. And for those who did wrong, a man to fear. Perhaps he was somewhat of a snob as far as his family was concerned. But that was because he wanted only the best for them.

And now he was dead. Why? Because someone feared him?

All this passed through my mind as I sat there on the chair in the large center hallway of Shadow Acres. And suddenly I realized I was staring at Bryan, unable to take in the facts of this awful tragedy. And Bryan was staring back at me, almost stupidly. Finally he asked, "Why did you come up here tonight?"

I looked away from him and caught sight of my face in a narrow mirror hanging on the opposite side of the hall. I looked deathly white — as white as Bryan was — only on my face the lipstick stood out ludicrously against the pallor of my skin. My brown eyes were like two large dark pools of horror. I pushed back my auburn bangs from my damp forehead. My fresh hairdo hadn't been helped by the dampness and the fog. "He phoned me also," I said tremulously, "to come at once — and alone!" My eyes opened wider. "Maybe it's suicide?" I suggested, my voice sounding husky and scared.

Bryan, who was still staring at me, heaved a heavy sigh. "Yes, yes, maybe it is," he agreed. "That's what it is — it's suicide." He seemed relieved at the thought. He stopped staring at me and looked down at the gun. "Strange," he muttered. "He was a queer man, and ruthless, to those who crossed him. But I wish he wasn't dead!" His voice ended in a choked sob.

Neither of us heard the front door open, and we both jumped nervously when a deep masculine voice said, "Well, this is one thing *I* won't be blamed for. Or will I?"

I whirled around. Gregory Sedgwick, the other grandson of the dead man, was standing in the doorway. He was wearing brown English tweeds, and his dark brown curly hair was matted to his forehead from the dampness. His face, darkly tanned for that time of the year, was lean and handsome; the finely chiseled lips were grim. His dark brown eyes, usually twinkling with humor, were flashing saber points of cutting light across the intervening space between him and Bryan.

My heart stood still for a split-second. I hadn't seen Greg since we'd broken our engagement during the big Donnybrook we'd had two years previous. The row had been the result of his being expelled from college in his senior year because a girl of questionable character had been found in his room. It had deeply hurt his grandfather, and the shock of his deliberate unfaithfulness to me had instantly killed my love for him. And as time passed, I'd grown to hate him as much as I'd previously loved him. Only my gradually dawning love for Bryan had finally healed the wound.

All I could do now was breathe, "Greg!" in a hushed voice.

Bryan was facing him, still holding the revolver. "What are *you* doing here?" he demanded fiercely. "And how do you know what has happened?"

There had always been a closeness between these two, a brotherly closeness, but now an enmity seemed to burst into vicious flame, threatening to devour them both. It shocked and frightened me.

Greg smiled mirthlessly, his eyes taking on an almost supernatural gleam in the dim light of the hall. "I came by the back way and looked in the library window as I passed and saw the corpse on the floor and *you* bending over it — with the gun in your hand!"

"You rat!" Bryan cried. "What are you insinuating? He killed himself!" He sprang at Greg, his free hand working with an uncontrollable desire to get at Greg's strong brown throat. I'd never seen him like that before. But before he could reach Greg, I jumped up and stepped between them. "Wait a minute, boys!" I said shakily. "This is no time to work out a family feud — if there is a family feud."

Greg smiled down at me grimly. "Granddad didn't kill himself," he said. "He wasn't that kind. You know that. Somebody killed him because he had too much on them." He looked at Bryan accusingly.

Bryan stopped, hesitating, looking down at the revolver in his hand in a puzzled way. There was some oil on his hand, and he wiped it off on his coat, heedless of the fact that he was wearing his new tuxedo and that the oil was leaving a greasy spot. Then he walked slowly back to the library and laid the gun on the desk. He reached for the phone, but before he could lift the receiver Greg shoved me aside and bounded into the room. Snatching the instrument, he cried, "Fool! We'll settle this between ourselves!"

Bryan's lips tightened. His gaze met Greg's. "You can't settle a murder without the police," he said quietly. "This is more than a family matter."

A chill slid over me, and I pulled my mink cape closer around me. Apparently he didn't believe it was suicide. Had Greg done it? I couldn't believe that.

Ever since I could remember, Greg had been getting into scrapes and Bryan had been making excuses for him. But even so, I had grown up loving the gay, carefree, happy-go-lucky Greg. He'd been my one and only love ever since childhood, until that last scrape. Now I loved Bryan. And Bryan must not suffer for this crime.

I walked slowly to the doorway of the library. I said, "Bryan, you shouldn't have touched the gun. Now your fingerprints will be on it."

He gave me a sudden look but made no move to wipe off the gun. "You're right," he agreed. "I shouldn't have. Professional criminals always wear gloves, don't they?" He tried to force a smile, but it was a dismal failure.

"Please don't joke," I pleaded. I was beginning to feel desperate.

Bryan, Greg and I had grown up together. The boys were both Mr. Sedgwick's grandsons. Mr. and Mrs. Sedgwick had had two boys. Bryan was the son of Robert, and Greg was the son of Gregory, Jr., making them cousins. My mother and father had been close friends of the Sedgwicks, and my father and Mr. Sedgwick were partners in a thriving law business. When my folks were alive, we'd had a house a few miles away from Shadow Acres, as had the two Sedgwick sons, and we visited back and forth regularly. As a matter of fact, Bryan and Greg had been like brothers to me, except that by the time we were grown up, Greg and I discovered we were in love with each other in a grown up way and subsequently became engaged.

Suddenly Bryan came toward me. "Say, Reda, *you* mustn't get mixed up in this!" he cried. "You must get out of here at once!" He reached me and put an arm around my shivering shoulders. "Come on, dear," he said. "I'll drive you home."

"Why not let *me* drive her home?" Greg asked. "I think I still remember the way."

I quickly swallowed a lump in my throat. Was he going to force himself on me, even after what had happened between us? I said, "I don't live up here any more. After Dad died last year I moved into the city. I have an apartment on East Eighty-First Street."

He raised his eyebrows. "Oh?" he said. The way he said it made me furious, and I wanted to strike him, to hurt him, the way he'd hurt me. But did I dare? What did he know about this murder, other than what he'd just told us? And was he telling the truth? Would he take this opportunity to satisfy his grudge against Bryan? Bryan has always been so good and honest, always excusing Greg for his carryings-on, always placating their grandfather when he became upset about one of Greg's escapades. Bryan had been spoiled, yes, but he'd always been

35

a good boy when it came to fundamental things.

I looked from one to the other. How could I ever have thought I loved Greg, when Bryan was so dear and sweet? I mustn't let Greg hurt Bryan now. I'd do anything — go away with Bryan, give up my music — anything.

Bryan was glaring at Greg. "Reda is engaged to *me* now," he said. "Her well-being is *my* responsibility."

I saw Greg flinch. "I heard about it," he said, his lips tight.

Bryan began to urge me toward the still open front door, but Greg quickly blocked our way. "Oh, no, you don't!" His words cracked like pistol shots. "You're not going to get away with *this* so easily!"

Bryan shook off his detaining arm. "I'll settle with you later," he said, shoving past Greg, his arm still around me.

But before we could step out the doorway, we were again stopped, this time by a policeman and a detective. "What's going on here?" the policeman asked, roughly pushing Bryan and me back into the hall.

Before either of us could speak, Greg sauntered toward us, his large brown hands deep in his trouser pockets, his dark, handsome face grim. "You tell them, Bryan," he

36

said. "You were the first one on the scene."

I gasped at the implication and flashed him a look of hate. Bryan let me go and swung on Greg, but he ducked effortlessly. "Some day I'll get you!" Bryan said between clenched teeth.

The policeman and detective looked speculatively from one to the other, then without a word went into the library. I could hear them talking in low tones to one another, but couldn't make out what they were saying. In a few minutes they came back into the hall. "We'll have to ask you folks a few questions," the detective said. "Can't we go into another room?"

"There's a living room across the hall here," Bryan said, leading the way, his arm again holding me close beside him. Greg followed. When we were all seated, the detective began his questions.

"Who discovered him first?" he asked.

"I did," Bryan said.

"Tell me all you know."

I fastened my eyes upon his face, scarcely daring to breathe. If anything happened to him, I wouldn't be able to stand it. In another week I would be his wife — *if* nothing happened. He was speaking, his voice warming my heart, even in the midst of this terrible tragedy. Why had we ever argued?

Why had I ever been apprehensive about our future together? He was a man now; not a spoiled child.

He told the same story he'd told me. The detective said, "Hum." Then he turned to me. I couldn't take my eyes from Bryan's white face. God grant he is telling the truth, I prayed silently. But of course he was. Bryan was the soul of honesty. But he *had* been holding the gun when I came in. I couldn't control the shiver that swept over me. I felt my face flush. I twisted my hands together nervously and dragged my eyes reluctantly from Bryan's face.

"He phoned me, too," I said. "He's my lawyer and an old family friend. He said he wanted to see me immediately, alone! When I got here —" I stopped suddenly. I couldn't say that when I arrived I'd found Bryan with the gun in his hands. Circumstantial evidence had convicted more than one man. I shuddered and chewed at my trembling lips.

"Come on," the detective said impatiently. "When you got here, *what?*"

"I rang the bell, but no one came to the door. It was unlocked, so I came in and —"

"Was *he* here when you arrived?" He nodded toward Bryan.

"Yes," I stammered.

"Go on; tell the truth," Bryan encouraged me.

"Don't interrupt," the policeman snapped. "Let her tell it in her own way."

"Where was he when you came in?" the detective asked me.

My eyes returned to Bryan, and he nodded for me to go on. "He was in the library," I said, scarcely above a whisper.

"You didn't hear a shot or anything, did you?" the detective asked.

I shook my head mutely.

The man turned to Gregory. "Now tell us what *you* know," he said, and I sighed with relief. I wasn't going to have to tell about the gun after all.

Greg smiled slightly. He'd been waiting for his chance. "Well," he said, slowly jingling change in his trouser pockets, "I've been away, down in Brazil, for two years. I came back on business yesterday. I have a sugar plantation down there. Thought I'd run out and see Granddad and tell him the —" he glanced at Bryan — "black sheep of the family had at last made good."

Bryan glared at him, but he continued his story. "I drove up the short cut that brings you to the back of the house, parked my car by the garage and walked around."

The policeman and the detective listened

patiently. "Then what?" the detective asked.

Greg continued. "At the library window, I looked in. I thought I'd surprise Granddad. He didn't know I was home." He drew in a deep breath, and his eyes swung to Bryan. "When I looked in the window I saw my cousin, Bryan, bending over something. He had a gun in his hand. I looked closer; then I saw —" He swallowed, stopped jingling the change in his trousers and, taking his right hand out of the pocket, ran it through his hair. He was apparently very emotionally upset. He said, "I saw Granddad. He was on the floor, where he is now, and it was very evident he was dead." He was controlling himself with an effort.

Bryan's eyes seemed to pierce him with darts of blue fire. "Where were you when Reda came in?" he demanded.

Greg met his eyes defiantly. "Coming in to confront you!" he said with venomous meaning. "But I saw Reda, and decided to wait."

There was more questioning, but nothing new was brought out. The detective phoned for the coroner, the photographers, the fingerprint man and all the rest of them; and Bryan, Greg and I were told to wait until the homicide squad arrived. In the meantime, the policeman went over the house and the detective went into the library.

I'd slipped off my fur cape and left it on one of the hall chairs. Bryan asked if he could phone the people who were giving the party for us and tell them we wouldn't be able to attend.

The detective grudgingly gave him permission. When he got Ruth Dana on the hall phone, he merely said his grandfather had died very suddenly and we wouldn't be able to come to the party.

There was nothing for us to do while we waited, and the time seemed interminable, although it couldn't have been more than half an hour.

Bryan went out to the dining room and fixed himself a drink. There was always a tray of assorted bottles of liquor and club soda on the sideboard and a thermos jug of ice cubes. He asked me if I wanted a drink, and I said, "No, thank you." He didn't ask Greg.

Greg paced the length of the living room several times, then stopped in front of me and stood looking down at me. After several minutes I asked, "Well?"

"You've changed," he said.

I shrugged. "So have you."

"You're older," he said.

41

I raised my eyebrows. "Two years older. I'll be twenty-one next week. When you went away I was nineteen."

A slight smile twitched his lips. "You're still pretty," he said, as if thinking aloud. "But some of the softness has gone. You're not exactly *hard* — perhaps *brittle* would be a better word."

I looked up at him, and a strange feeling flashed through me as our eyes met. "Perhaps what you mean is that I'm not as gullible as I used to be. I've learned to face facts."

His jaw tensed, and for a moment he looked like his grandfather with the two lines down each side of his mouth. "That's fortunate," he said, "because before this thing is over, I'm afraid you are going to have to face some very unpleasant ones."

I looked away and let my eyes rest on Bryan, who was now standing in the hall, sipping a long amber-colored drink and doing something to the thermostat, which was on the wall just at the foot of the stairs. I said, "Please go away, Greg, and let me alone."

"Very well," he said, and turned away. He went out into the hall just as the quiet of the house was split by the ear-piercing sirens of the homicide squad arriving.

Chapter Three

After the entire homicide squad arrived, there was no chance for Greg, Bryan or me to talk to one another. We were questioned again, together and separately; then we were finger-printed. What went on in the library we were not allowed to see.

When I saw them taking the body of Mr. Sedgwick out of the house, I began to cry. Bryan insisted I swallow some of his drink, and Greg just stood and watched us, his mouth grim, his hands clenched. They were both tall men and equally matched physi-cally, with broad shoulders, narrow hips and hard muscles. They were men to be proud of; men any girl could love. Or that was the way it seemed to me as I stood between them.

In the midst of it all John and Agnes came in. When they heard what had happened, they just stood and stared at us. After a while Agnes said, "It can't be true. Things like that don't happen at Shadow Acres!" She was a woman of somewhere around forty-five or fifty, sturdy without being heavy, of medium height, with a plain, honest face and graying black hair and brown eyes.

John was a few years older than she, tall and thin, with sandy hair and faded blue eyes. He seemed speechless until a policeman began to question him. Then he gave monsyllabic answers.

The policeman asked, "Was your employer here when you and your wife went out?"

"No."

"What time did you leave?"

"About ten this morning."

"Where did you go?"

"To the city."

"What did you do there?"

"We went to Radio City. Then we had dinner at some place near there and got the 10:30 train home."

"That seems to have given you a lot of time to do other things."

"We wandered around. My wife likes to window shop."

"Did anyone you know see you?"

He shrugged. "Not unless the conductors on the trains remember seeing us."

"We can try that. Can you drive a car?"

"Yes, sir."

"How many cars does — did your employer have?"

"Two."

"What kind?"

"A Cadillac and a Chevy station wagon."

"Did he ever let you use either of them?"

"Sometimes. The station wagon."

"You don't have a car of your own?"

"No, sir."

"And you didn't use the station wagon today?"

"No, sir. I never use it to go to the city. Just around here."

"How did you get to the train this morning?"

"There's a bus passes on the main road. About a ten minute walk."

"How did you get back from the station tonight?"

"Taxi."

"Had you any trouble with your employer?"

"Oh, no, sir."

"Had your wife?"

"No, sir. Mr. Sedgwick was very nice to work for."

"How long have you worked for him?"

"About fifteen years."

"Did he have any enemies?"

"Oh, no, sir."

"And did he get along with his family?"

"Oh, yes, sir. That is, you know how it is, all families have their little disagreements."

"Anything specific?"

"Not that I know of, sir."

"Was there ever any violence?"

"Oh, no, sir. It was always just talk. Sometimes kind of loud. But just talk."

"And didn't you ever hear what it was about?"

"No sir. I never listened. It was none of my business."

That was about all. I didn't hear Agnes being questioned, but as far as I could judge she told the same story.

Then Bryan, Greg and I were told we could go home but were to stay where we would be available. And we must be at the inquest the day after tomorrow, which would be Saturday.

Greg said, "I'd come out here planning to stay with my grandfather a few days. Is there any reason why I can't stay — at least until after the inquest and the funeral?"

The policeman in charge said, "No, I guess not."

Bryan said, "If he stays, I'm going to stay, too!"

He was very belligerent about it.

The police officer shrugged. "Okay. There will be a police guard around the house — just in case."

Everybody was suddenly looking at me. A policeman asked, "Do you want a police escort home, miss? Or are you going to stay, too?"

I looked from Bryan to Greg. Greg's eyes met mine, and there was a challenge in them. Bryan said, "I'd feel better if you went home, Reda."

I didn't know what to do. I would have preferred to go home and get away from that house that had suddenly become so menacing and unfriendly. But I couldn't leave Greg and Bryan there together, in their present frame of mind. Even with John, Agnes and a police guard, I didn't like the idea of their being there together. I said, "I think I'll stay. Agnes will fix rooms for all of us."

Chapter Four

Agnes prepared my usual room for me, and Bryan and Greg had rooms on the other side of the house.

Agnes and John had a suite of rooms on the third floor: a living room, bedroom and bath, which were reached by a back staircase that went up from just beside the kitchen. There was no access to the third floor from any other part of the house.

The room I always used when I visited Shadow Acres was large, with a bay window overlooking the back gardens and lawns. It was furnished in mahogany, with a four-poster canopy bed, a bonnet-topped highboy and several comfortable chairs with a couple of small tables. There was a large walk-in closet, and opening from the side of the room was a small, nicely appointed bathroom. The color scheme was apple green with accents of gold. The woodwork was white.

Not having any night clothes with me, I realized I would have to sleep in my bra and briefs, but there were plenty of bedcovers, so I would be warm enough.

I'd brought my mink cape upstairs, and after I'd put out my lights I threw it around me and went over and opened one of the windows. Even in the winter, I had to have air in the room when I slept. For a moment I stood looking out. The fog swirling around the huge trees that surrounded the house gave an eerie effect, and it was impossible to see the gardens or lawns. It was from the large old trees that Shadow Acres got its name. Usually I like trees, but tonight they seemed menacing as their dark forms hid behind the fog.

I'd spent a great deal of time in this house during my almost twenty-one years of life — most of them pleasant, although as my memory traveled back through the years I remembered some times that had been not so pleasant.

There was the time when I was five. My mother, father and I had come to spend Christmas with Mr. and Mrs. Sedgwick. The two Sedgwick boys were there also, with their wives and children.

Robert Sedgwick, Bryan's father, was tall and thin, with blond hair and blue eyes. He was a serious type of man, a loan cashier of a small bank in one of the nearby towns.

His wife, Sybil, was very much like him:

tall and slender, rather pretty but without much personality. She was also blond and blue-eyed, and she was an echo of her husband. She was the "Yes, dear" kind — if you know what I mean.

Their son, Bryan, now my fiancé, was an active child, six at the time of the Christmas I was thinking about. He was into everything, and as I remember it, I didn't like him very much. For one thing, he threw my teddy bear into the fire in the living room and then laughed when I cried. His mother said, "Why, Bryan, you bad boy!" But she did nothing to punish him. She never did punish him, no matter what he did.

My mother was very annoyed and took me on her lap to comfort me, saying, "Never mind, darling. We'll get a new teddy bear the next time we go down to the city."

But that wasn't what I wanted. I wanted my old teddy bear that had slept with me ever since someone had given it to me on my second birthday.

Bryan asked his mother, "Why is she crying so much just for an old teddy bear?" And his mother had said, "Because she's a girl. Girls are cry babies."

"They are nothing of the kind!" my mother said.

"Everybody cries if they have a good

reason to — girls *and* boys, and even men and women."

"I've never seen Robert cry," Sybil said. "A *real* man doesn't cry!"

Greg, then seven, had been sitting on the floor playing with some new trains his grandfather had given him for Christmas. Looking up at his Aunt Sybil, he said, "*I* cry. And so does Bryan. I've seen him."

Sybil said, "No one asked for your opinion. Children should be seen and not heard."

Everyone else was either in another part of the house or outside, so we four were alone in the room. Greg glowered at his aunt. "I don't have to pay any attention to you!" he said.

Sybil got to her feet, put an arm around Bryan and said, "Come on, son; let's go out for a walk."

After they'd gone, Greg came over to me. "I have a teddy bear," he said. "You can have it if you want it. I'm getting too big for it anyway."

I remember throwing my arms around his neck and giving him a kiss. "I like you, Greg," I said, a smile chasing away the tears. And I think it was at that moment that I began to love him.

Greg backed away. "Well, gee! You don't have to *kiss* me!" he said.

51

My mother laughed. "Maybe Greg would let you play with his trains," she suggested.

"Sure. Come on. Just don't cry any more. And don't *kiss* me!"

Greg's father was quite different from his brother Robert; more like his own father. He was tall and well built, with brown hair and eyes. He was Gregory Sedgwick, Junior, and *his* father was Gregory Sedgwick, Senior. *My* Greg (I still think of him as *my* Greg, even now) was Gregory III.

The elder Gregory Sedgwick hadn't approved of his son's marriage, although he was always nice to his daughter-in-law. She was on the stage, a musical comedy star. She sang and danced and, as I remember her, was the most beautiful thing I had ever seen. She looked the way I imagined an angel should look. But according to the family gossip, always passed around in whispers, she was no angel.

Greg was twelve when his mother and father were divorced, and soon after, Natalie married her leading man and Greg was sent away to school, because his father didn't want to leave him entirely with servants.

After that I saw him only in the summers and during school holidays through the year. During those times he used to visit with us, his Aunt Sybil and Uncle Robert, and sometimes came to Shadow Acres, where Agnes and John looked after him after his grandmother died.

It was after his mother and father were divorced that Greg began getting into trouble. After that he and Bryan seemed to draw closer together and began being real pals. Everybody thought it was a good thing for Greg, because Bryan was much a nice boy. I did, too, only it meant I didn't see Greg as often as I used to. They had reached the age where they didn't want to be bothered with girls, so I was shunted off for several years, during which there was the time when Greg stole the bicycle of one of the boys at school. He never would say why, because he had a bicycle of his own, but when the police began looking for the stolen bicycle it was found in Greg's garage. That was while he and his father were still living in their house, after the divorce.

Greg was stubborn and wouldn't answer the questions of the police, nor would he talk to his father about it. Sometimes I wondered if he'd borrowed it for Bryan because Bryan didn't have one. But when I asked him, he was cross and told me to mind my own business.

Then there was the time some money was missing from the purse of a visitor who was having tea with Bryan's mother. Her hat, coat and purse were on the guest room bed, and the boys were playing up in Bryan's room across the hall.

When the loss was discovered, there was a great to-do, and the maid and the boys were questioned. But each denied knowing anything about it. A few days later Bryan began buying candy and a baseball mitt and several other things his parents knew he didn't have the money for. When they questioned him, he said Greg had bought them for him. And when Greg was questioned, he admitted he had.

While they were in college, there were several things that got Greg into trouble. Once the car belonging to a boy in Greg's class was taken and smashed up, and it turned out Greg had been driving it. Another time, an examination paper disappeared the night before the exam and was found in Greg's room. And there were other things of lesser importance.

Each time the trouble was smoothed over, and Greg's natural charm and promise to do better saved him from too severe punishment. But when the girl was found in his room, scantily clad, that was the last straw — for everybody.

Through it all my love for him had lasted.

He always had a way of making a joke of everything so it was impossible to get angry with him, and by that time we had just naturally drifted into our engagement. I was so in love with him I was ready to forgive him everything — everything but that last episode.

When I was with him, I couldn't imagine him doing the things he did. He wasn't the renegade type. And each time I heard of his doing something, I always used to say, "I can't believe it. It's not like Greg to do a thing like that!"

And so time went on, and all of us, Bryan, Greg and I, grew up to be what we are today.

My own father and mother were my ideal people. Both were tall, slender, and to me beautiful. My mother had red-brown hair with a slight wave, and eyes the color of cream sherry. Her skin was fair and her teeth perfect and very white, and when she smiled a dimple appeared in her right cheek. I'm happy to say I have the same dimple and the same coloring, only my hair is redder and my eyes darker; more like my father's. My mother had been a teacher of music in a private school when she met my father, who at the time was just starting with the law firm of Sedgwick & Sedgwick.

The firm of Sedgwick & Sedgwick had

originally been composed of old Mr. Sedgwick and his father, and when his father died he kept the firm name because the dream of his life had been to have his two boys grow up to be lawyers and enter the firm with him. But as it turned out, neither boy was interested in law. Bryan's father preferred banking, and Greg's father wanted to be a newspaper man — and became one, eventually becoming an overseas correspondent.

This being the case, the elder Sedgwick began to pin his hopes on his grandsons. When neither of them showed any interest in the law, he turned his attention to my father, who had come into the firm right from college. As the years passed, the two men became close friends in spite of the differences in their ages, and when I was fifteen, Bryan sixteen and Greg seventeen, he made my father a partner and the name of the firm was changed to Sedgwick & Randall, my father's name being Richard Randall.

As all this had been going through my mind I had been standing before the opened window with nothing on but my bra, briefs and the waist-length fur cape, and I began to realize the combination was not enough protection against the cold wind blowing in the partially opened window. I started to turn away and get into bed; taking a last look, I noticed the wind was blowing away the fog and a half-moon was breaking through the clouds and mist, casting shadows on the gardens and lawns. As I watched, I thought I saw a darker shadow moving at the far side of the back lawn. I decided it must be one of the policemen guarding the house. But a policeman wouldn't be that shape. What I was watching was definitely the shape of a woman, in a woman's clothing.

But it couldn't be. Agnes wouldn't be out at this time of night, at least not so far from the house. And she and I were the only women on the place that night. And Shadow Acres had no near neighbors.

Oh, well, I'd probably just imagined it.

Slipping off my fur cape, I dropped it down on a chair and got into bed, glad of the soft blanket and comforter to warm my chilled body.

Snapping off the bedside lamp, I closed my eyes. I was very tired. Sleep should claim me very soon. And it did. But suddenly, in the midst of a lovely dream about my parents and Greg, I was awakened.

My heart thumping, I listened. Surely those were footsteps out in the hall. But so what? Probably Greg or Bryan couldn't sleep and had decided to go downstairs for a drink or something to eat. Or perhaps one of the policemen was on guard inside the house and periodically making the rounds to be sure everything was all right.

With a sigh I closed my eyes and settled myself for sleep again. I'd almost made it when I heard men's voices raised as if in anger.

I opened my eyes and sat up, snapped on the bedside light and listened. Then I got out of bed and went to the door and opened it a crack. There was very definitely an argument going on between two men, and as I listened I was able to identify the voices of Bryan and Greg. They were downstairs, probably in the library.

I grabbed my cape and, covering the front of me with it as best I could, ran barefoot down the stairs.

There was a light in the library, and Greg and Bryan were standing in front of the desk, Bryan in his underwear with just shoes on his feet, and Greg in tan pajamas and a dark red robe and slippers, which he must have had in his car. The two were practically coming to blows.

I ran over to the door and cried, "Stop it! What's the matter with you, both of you!

What are you doing down here in the middle of the night?"

The argument stopped, and both men turned to look at me. They were both speechless now, both staring at me as if I were an apparition. Then, with a sudden twinkle in his eyes, Greg said, "Oh, it's you."

Bryan just stood staring at me. Then Greg, his face breaking into a grin, said, "Turn around."

Realizing what my rear view must be, I felt myself blush, and Greg began to laugh. But Bryan didn't. Coming toward me, he said, "Get out of here! Go upstairs!"

I hugged my cape closer. It covered me from my chin to my knees — in the front. "I won't!" I said. "What are you two fighting about?"

Greg, sobering suddenly, said, "Grand-dad's will."

"It's probably down in his office in the city," I told him.

Bryan began opening and closing the desk drawers, pulling out papers indiscriminately. "I'm sure he kept a copy here," he said. His hair was disheveled, and he looked as if he'd had too much to drink.

Greg went over to him and yanked him away from the desk. "Even if there is a copy of it here somewhere, it's none of your business. We'll know what's in it soon enough!"

Bryan gave him a shove. "I want to know now. I want to know where I stand so I can make plans."

I went into the room and sat down on the nearest chair. "But why? What difference does it make?" I asked. Then I began to shiver, and not entirely from the chill of the room. "Bryan," I said, "you're not yourself. You're drunk!" Tears came to my eyes and began running down my cheeks. "Oh, Bryan!" I cried. "How *could* you? How *can* you act like this so soon after —" I let the rest of my sentence trail off into silence.

The front door opened and a policeman came in. "What's going on here?" he demanded. "Why aren't you folks in bed?"

I began to feel conscious of my lack of adequate clothing. "We were," I said. "But — well, we got up again." I got to my bare feet but realized I couldn't very well leave the room, thereby exposing my back.

Greg, realizing my predicament, came over to me and, adroitly taking the cape from my shaking hands, said, "Make a quick turn, and I'll hold the cape so your rear end is covered. And don't worry about what *I* see. Remember, I've seen you in a bikini more than once."

"Keep your hands off her!" Bryan yelled, and made a leap for us. But the policeman stepped in front of him and stopped him. "Take it easy," he advised him. "The lady seems to be in good hands."

Greg grinned at him and, keeping my rear carefully covered with the cape, got me out into the hall, closing the library door behind us. Then, handing me the cape, he said, "Now scoot. Up to bed. And stay there. And lock your door."

As I ran up the stairs, completely vulnerable to his gaze, which I instinctively knew would be admiring, I said over my shoulder, "There isn't any key."

"Then put a chair against it."

I nodded and hurried up the rest of the stairs, down the hallway and into the room, closing the door and leaning against it. I was thoroughly shaken, but not from what had happened down in the library. I was shaken because I realized I was beginning to feel the old attraction of Greg pulling at my heartstrings.

But I mustn't let that happen. Greg and I were through. And goodness knew how many girls he'd had down in Brazil.

Chapter Five

When I got back into bed, shivering, I knew I wouldn't sleep any more that night. Besides, the night was almost over. In the far distance a rooster was greeting the first streaks of dawn, and crows were calling to one another: "Caw, caw, caw." Then the answer from far off: "Caw, caw, caw, caw." I began to count the caws. There was always three from the first crow and then four in answer from his friend, relative or a new acquaintance.

After a while I heard Bryan and Greg come upstairs. They weren't talking. Then I heard their bedroom doors close; one softly, the other with a bang. The bang was probably Bryan.

I must have dozed off after that, because the next thing I knew someone was tapping on my door. With an effort I roused myself enough to ask, "Who is it?"

"It's me. Agnes."

I stretched and yawned and managed to say, "Oh! Well, come in."

The door opened, and Agnes entered with my breakfast tray. Over one arm she had a

62

dress. Setting the tray down on a table, she said, "I took the liberty of bringing you one of my dresses. It is freshly cleaned, and I remembered that last night you were wearing an evening dress. You won't want to put that on this morning."

I sat up in bed, and she fixed the pillows behind me. "No," I said, "I suppose not. Thank you, Agnes. That was very thoughtful of you."

She brought my breakfast tray and placed it on my legs. "The dress will be a little large for you, but I think I can pin it so it won't look too bad. It's a little tight for me."

"Thank you, Agnes," I said. I noticed my breakfast consisted of orange juice, toast and coffee. At the back of the tray was a folded newspaper. I reached for it, but before I could open it Agnes said, "Maybe I shouldn't have brought you the paper but — well, John and I talked it over and decided you'd have to know sometime."

My heart began to pound and my hands shook as I opened the paper. Then I gasped. The headline read:

GRANDSON OF SEDGWICK
ACCUSES COUSIN OF MURDER

My hands trembled so I had to lay the

paper on the bed beside me while I read the details. "Oh, but he didn't — not actually!" I cried. Then I began to read the story.

"It was not explained what had been in the old gentleman's mind when he phoned Miss Reda Randall, his ward, and his grandson, Bryan Sedgwick, to come to see him. And even more strange was the fact, disclosed by the police, that he had also called the local police to send someone up at about eight-fifteen. What had been his plan? Or fear? Had he committed suicide after first summoning the two people who would be most interested? But the police report that the only fingerprints on the gun are those of his grandson, Bryan."

As I read the printed words, I felt as if an icy hand were clutching my heart.

"An early arrest is expected," the paper proclaimed.

Would it be Bryan? Could he prove his innocence? Would I be forced to testify that he had met me with the gun in his hand? Would Greg testify he'd seen him with the gun in his hand? But he'd have to. He'd already said that.

Personally, I'd never been good at lying. I'd be sure to break down under the cross-questioning of a ruthless and clever district attorney.

Agnes, puttering around the room, closing the window, straightening the curtains, said, "It's a terrible thing. But he never committed suicide. Not him."

I tried to eat my breakfast but was only able to manage the orange juice and part of the coffee. "How can you be sure?" I asked her.

She came over and stood beside the bed, and I caught a faint whiff of a cheap toilet water — gardenia. "Because I knew him," she said. "He enjoyed living too much. And —" she took the breakfast tray away so I could get up "— he was looking forward to seeing you and Mr. Bryan get married. He said he'd always wanted a daughter, and he felt as if you were going to take the place of the one he'd never had."

I got out of bed, my eyes full of sudden tears. "He was always very good to me," I said as I hurried over to the bathroom.

When Agnes saw me in my bra and briefs, she said, "For heaven sakes! Why didn't I think to bring you a nightdress?"

"It didn't matter," I assured her. As she started for the hall door with the tray, she said, "I'll be back by the time you finish your bath. And I'll bring some safety pins for the dress."

I took a warm shower and put my bra and

brief back on. I always put on fresh underwear each morning, and again later, if I
dressed to go out. I disliked using these
things I'd worn not only last evening, but
slept in all night. Well — worn all night,
since I hadn't slept all night.

Agnes was waiting for me when I came
out of the bathroom. She helped me into the
dress and cleverly arranged it around the
waist, pinning it in pleats and then covering
the pins with the belt.

It was a tailored, shirtwaist-type dress in a
dark brown linen, and when she got through
with it, it didn't look too badly on me, except that it was too long. But Agnes quickly
remedied that. She'd brought a needle and a
spool of brown thread as well as the pins and
in no time she'd basted the hem so it was
just the right length.

"There," she said. "Not the latest thing
from Paris, but better than an evening
dress for a day at Shadow Acres, especially with those policemen coming and
going."

I said, "Thank you, Agnes. You're a doll."
Then I asked, "Are the police still here?"

"Not right now. I gave them some breakfast, and then they went away. But there's no
telling when they'll be back."

"I didn't know Mr. Sedgwick had asked

the police to be here at eight-fifteen last night. Did you?"

Agnes grunted. "I didn't know any of you were going to be here." Then, changing the subject, she said, "I guess you'll have to wear your evening slippers, whether you like it or not. My feet are too big for you to wear any of my shoes, unless you want to put both feet in one shoe and hop."

I laughed. "No thanks," I said, and began to put on my sheer stockings and the light blue satin strap sandals that matched my evening dress. "I guess nobody will notice my feet anyway," I decided.

"Nobody but Mr. Greg. He don't miss anything about you."

I felt my face flush and kept leaning over, pretending to have trouble fastening the straps on the slippers, so she wouldn't see me blushing. "You're thinking of the old days," I mumbled. "Things are different now. I scarcely know Greg — any more."

Agnes began to make the bed. "Suppose you'll have to postpone your wedding now?" she asked, her back to me.

I began to do something with my hair. I had only the small comb from my vanity that I had in a lining pocket of my fur cape, but I managed to get the snarls out and fix it so at least it didn't look as if I'd just gotten out of bed.

I said, "Yes, I guess so. We'll have to wait and see what happens."

Agnes fluffed up a pillow. "Do you think they'll arrest Mr. Bryan?"

I walked over to the window and stood looking out. "I hope not. I'm sure he didn't do it." There was no sun, and the gardens and lawns looked bleak and frozen. I tried to figure out why a woman would have been over on the far side of the back lawn last night and decided she could have been coming from or going to the back way by which Greg had arrived.

Agnes threw the spread over the bed and began smoothing it. "But he *did* have the gun in his hand?" she persisted.

I put a hand up to my throat, which suddenly had developed a big, aching lump. "Yes, but that doesn't mean anything."

Agnes sighed. "No, it doesn't. And I don't believe he'd shoot his grandfather. His father was a rotter, but the boy has always seemed to be all right."

I whirled around and faced her. "What do you mean — his father was a rotter?"

She stood looking at me, her hands on her hips, the bed finished. "You mean you didn't know?"

68

"Know what?" I demanded. "I always thought Bryan's father was a paragon of virtue."

Agnes said, "Ha! He even made passes at me. And one time John nearly punched him in the nose."

I had to choke back a hysterical laugh. "Oh no! Agnes, you can't mean that!"

"I do indeed. And you needn't laugh. I used to be good-looking when I was younger."

I didn't know what to say. But there wasn't really anything but the obvious, so I said it. "I'm sure you were, Agnes. And you're still nice-looking."

She turned away and went to the hall door. "Well, I'm sorry if I talked out of turn. But I thought you knew."

"No harm done," I told her as she went out. But there had been harm done. She had, with one stroke, killed all my childish illusions. If Bryan's father hadn't been what I'd always thought him to be — had anybody?

I began to think back to my childhood. Agnes and John must have been young then. I tried to remember what they looked like and eventually got a vague picture of a nice-looking maid who used to bake cookies and cakes for us kids when we came to visit

Mr. and Mrs. Sedgwick. As I remembered her, she had thick, straight black hair and wore it in braids around her head. I can remember the little maid's cap perching on top of the braids and often wobbling ludicrously if she didn't pin it on tightly enough.

She had large, dark eyes and an ivory skin with a faint rose petal coloring that came and went as she talked. A typical Irish type. Beneath her neat uniforms there was a very good figure, and I remember Robert Sedgwick saying one time, as she left the room after having brought tea, "Best-looking legs I ever saw."

His mother had said, "Hush! She'll hear you!" And his wife Sybil said, "Robert!" That was all; just, "Robert!" But it was enough. Sometimes the worm turned.

Then I began to remember other things I'd thought I'd forgotten. I remembered one time when Bryan had been sick. I think he had chicken pox, and I was allowed to visit him because I'd already had it. It was a Sunday afternoon, and I was up in his room playing Parcheesi with him. Sybil had gone out somewhere for tea or something. Robert, who had not wanted to go, was downstairs in the living room reading and waiting for Sybil to return so he could drive me home.

After a while the back doorbell rang, and I heard Robert walk through the hall to answer it. Their maid had Sunday off after an early one o'clock dinner. After Robert had opened the door, I could hear men's voices. Gradually they were raised in an argument. "Who is that?" I asked Bryan.

"How should I know?"

"But it sounds almost like a fight!" We stopped our game and listened and heard Robert say, "Now you listen to me, John; don't you ever dare to say anything like that to me again or I'll have you fired — you and Agnes both."

Bryan and I looked at each other and, as I remember it, we were both not only surprised but scared.

"If you try it," John yelled, "I'll tell what I know about you forcing yourself on Miss Natalie!"

"Why, you — !" There was a scuffle, then John's voice again. "You're a hypocrite, Robert Sedgwick!" he yelled. "Butter wouldn't melt in your mouth when the family are around. But the minute you get alone with a woman, you —"

There was another scuffle; then John yelled, "And you let my wife alone!" Then the door banged, and Robert stamped back to the living room. After that there was silence until Sybil returned a half-hour later. I wondered if that was the time John had almost punched Robert in the nose.

For a few moments after the door had banged, Bryan and I had looked at each other. I asked, "What did he mean?" Bryan began vigorously to shake the dice in the round black cardboard box. "Nothing. My father just tries to be nice to people, and they don't understand." His little red-spotted hand was gripping the dice box as if he were afraid it would get away from him, and I, embarrassed but not understanding why, giggled and said, "Your turn."

After that we played doggedly, but neither of us enjoyed it, and I was glad when Sybil came back and, after talking to her husband a few minutes, came to the foot of the stairs and called, "I'll run you home now, Reda. Uncle Robert isn't feeling well."

When I went downstairs, the door to the living room was closed and I didn't see Uncle Robert, as I called him. And I promptly forgot the entire episode, because when I got home, I found Greg and his mother and father had stopped in for a while, and Greg and I went outside and played on my rustic gym, which consisted of a swing, a couple of ladders for climbing, and a seesaw.

Strange that I'd so completely forgotten that Sunday afternoon until now. That is, I'd forgotten the part at Bryan's house. I had never forgotten a moment I ever spent with Greg.

Chapter Six

Getting back to the present, as soon as I finished dressing that morning after the tragedy at Shadow Acres, I went downstairs. Greg was in the library, sitting at his grandfather's desk. He was looking through the morning paper.

I went into the room and sat down near him, saying, "Good morning," as I crossed the room.

He looked at me over the top of the paper. "Oh, good morning, chicken," he said.

I felt my heart jerk. "Chicken" had always been his pet name for me.

"Get any sleep?" he asked, folding the paper and putting it down on the desk.

"A little. Not much. Did you?"

"Not much. I had a lot of thinking to do."

I said, "Yes, I guess we all did." Then impulsively I said, "Greg, we've got to stick together on this."

"What do you mean?"

"I mean — you and Bryan and me."

"Don't we always? Or nearly always?" His eyes met mine, and I couldn't turn mine away. It was so long since Greg and I had looked into each other's eyes it made me feel weak.

"You didn't have to accuse Bryan last night!" I said.

He took his eyes from mine and let them wander to one of the windows through which the frozen side garden could be seen. "I didn't accuse him. I just told the truth. Besides, a fellow can accumulate a lot of venom in two lonely years. And when I saw you with him, some of it spilled out."

"Some of it? You mean there's more?"

He swung his eyes from the window back to me and smiled very faintly. "There's lots more of it, chicken. But don't let it worry you. I won't do or say anything to hurt you."

I flounced in my chair. "Stop calling me 'chicken,' " I snapped crossly.

His smile broadened, and his eyebrows rose questioningly. "Bring back old memories?" he asked.

I looked down at my hands, which were tightly clasped in my lap, because I didn't want him to see the quick tears in my eyes. "Perhaps," I said. "Memories that are best forgotten."

He shook his head. "No — not forgotten. Things that have been pleasant should never be forgotten."

I looked up at him. "Don't tell me you've become a philosopher?"

He made a rueful face at me. "No, not that. But I had a lot of time to think, down there in Brazil, and I realized that I'd been a fool to go off and leave you."

I stared at him. "You didn't have much choice, did you?" I sat up straight and, unclasping my hands, gripped the chair arms with them.

He leaned back in his grandfather's chair, and it tilted slightly. It was one of those swivel chairs that tilt when you lean back. Clasping his hands behind his head, he said, "I could have stayed and fought it out."

"But you don't think I —"

He sighed. "I don't think you'd have believed me if I'd said I wasn't guilty — no. I'm sure you wouldn't have. But if I'd stayed around, you might eventually have forgiven me."

I jumped to my feet and started for the door. "I won't stay here and listen to such nonsense!" I cried, my breath quickening as my heart began to beat faster.

He got up leisurely but managed to reach the door first. Standing before me, he put his hands on my shoulders and looked down into my face. "Do you really love Bryan?" he asked.

I tried to pull away from him, but his hands held me too tightly. "Of course I do," I said, refusing to look at him.

"As much as you used to love me?"

I felt a sob rising within me and struggled to free myself. "More!" I cried. "Much more!"

He pulled me close to him and held me so I could feel his heart beating — as turbulently as my own. "I don't believe it, chicken," he said softly. "I just don't believe it." He kissed the top of my head, and I put my face against his shoulder and started to cry silently.

That was the way Bryan found us when he came downstairs, dressed in his tuxedo trousers and a brown wool plaid shirt of his grandfather's which was too large for him.

"What the — !" he cried, and rushed at us like a raging bull.

Greg let me go but managed to get and keep hold of one of my hands. "The shock is catching up with her," he said casually. "She shouldn't have stayed here last night. Perhaps you can get her quieted down." Gently he pushed me toward Bryan and walked out of the room and in the direction of the kitchen.

It took me several minutes to get myself under control. I covered my face with my hands — the one Greg had been holding was still warm from his — and for some silly reason it was comforting.

Bryan stood looking at me for a moment, then came to me and put his arms around me. "There, there," he said. "Don't cry like that." I stood stiff and unresponsive within the circle of his arms until I was able to stop the tears; then I pulled away from him. "I have to get a handkerchief or a Kleenex or something," I stammered, and ran out of the room and up the stairs.

There was a box of tissues in my bathroom, and I dried my tears and blew my nose, wandering over to one of the bedroom windows as I did so. Looking out, I saw Greg, hands rammed in his trouser pockets, walking around the garden. He was looking down at the ground as if in deep thought. Watching him, I noticed how broad his shoulders were. But at the moment they sagged, and he had a defeated look that tore at my heart. He was wearing the same brown tweed suit he'd had on last night, but he'd changed his shirt and tie, and the tie was one I'd given him several years ago for Christmas. Had he chosen to wear it today deliberately? Or was it just one of his favorites? Surely he had no idea he would see me while he was visiting Shadow Acres.

What would his grandfather's death mean to him? I wondered. Would he be one of the heirs? Or had his grandfather disowned him after that fracas in college two years ago, as Bryan had said, and left everything to Greg's father or to Bryan? If Greg had made good financially down in Brazil with his sugar plantation, then the money wouldn't be important to him. Probably he was just feeling badly about losing his grandfather. I knew he had been very fond of him. Or perhaps he was upset by seeing me? But I was being conceited to have a thought like that.

I wondered why Bryan had been so anxious to find his grandfather's will last night, and if he had eventually found it in the desk after I'd gone upstairs. This morning he seemed to have forgotten his frenzy of the wee small hours. I wondered if he would, as he'd predicted, inherit Shadow Acres.

I went downstairs again and out to the kitchen. Agnes was there alone. I said, "Agnes, were you out in the back garden last night, after we all went upstairs?"

She turned toward me from the stove, where she'd been stirring something. "No," she said, surprised at my question. "Why should I be?"

"I don't know. I just wondered. I was looking out the window after I got undressed, and I thought I saw a woman at the far side of the back lawn, near the short cut to the back road."

She turned back to the stove. "Probably one of the policemen," she said.

"No. It wasn't a man. It was a woman."

Agnes shrugged. "You were upset. You were imagining things."

I sighed and went out of the kitchen and wandered into the living room. There was a grand piano in a far corner, and I went over and sat down and began to play softly. I'd often played on this piano, and it was soothing to feel the keys beneath my fingers. I began to play Claude Debussy's "*Clair de lune*" and the "*Deux Arabesques.*" They had always been favorites of mine. From them I went into a Chopin waltz.

I had almost come to the end of the waltz when I glanced up and saw Greg lounging in a chair by the door. I stopped, startled. I hadn't noticed him come in.

"Don't stop," he said. "I always enjoyed hearing you play."

I jumped up. "I've finished," I said, and started for the door. But I had to pass him to get out of the room, and as I did so he reached out and caught my arm, stopping me. "Wait a minute," he said. "I want to talk to you."

I tried to pull away, but he wouldn't let me. "I don't want to talk to *you!*" I said.

He sat up in his chair; then he got to his feet, still holding onto me. "I was thinking," he said. "Suppose I say I killed Granddad? Would that make it easier for you?"

I whirled around to face him. "But you didn't!" I cried, feeling suddenly breathless.

"How do you know? I could have done it before either you or Bryan arrived."

"But your fingerprints weren't on the gun."

"I could have worn gloves."

"Then there would be oil on them," I said, remembering the conversation Bryan and I had had about that very thing.

He raised one eyebrow. "And if you could find those gloves and take them to the police —"

I stared up into his face. "Are you crazy?" I cried. "Do you think for one minute I'd do that to you? Besides, playing the martyr isn't your type."

His hand tightened on my arm for a moment; then he let me go. With a deep sigh he said, "It was just a thought."

"Where is Bryan?" I asked him.

He shrugged. "I don't know. He has a habit of disappearing."

A police car drove up and stopped in front

of the house, and two policemen got out. Greg said, "You go up to your room. I'll take care of them."

I started to obey him, then turned to the foot of the stairs. "Greg," I said, "don't do anything foolish."

He smiled at me, and our eyes met and held for a moment. "I won't, chicken," he promised. "From here on in, it's every man for himself. Now quick, get upstairs and stay out of sight."

I did as he told me, closing the door to my room and sinking down on a soft, comfortable chair.

I was feeling very confused. Greg's effect on me was too strong just to shrug it off. I'd thought I'd put him out of my heart for good. But seeing him again, hearing his voice, feeling his arms about me, had brought everything back in a rushing torrent that was threatening to engulf me.

I put my head back and closed my eyes. I was awfully tired. I hadn't slept more than a couple of hours at most during the night.

I must have gone to sleep, because the next thing I knew someone was knocking on my door. I pulled myself awake and asked, "Who is it?"

"It's me, Bryan. Let me in." There was urgency in his voice.

I sat up. "The door isn't locked," I called. "There isn't a key to it. Come on in."

He flung the door open and catapulted into the room, slamming the door shut behind him. "Do you know where Greg is?" he demanded.

"No. The last time I saw him he was just about to open the front door to a couple of policemen."

"But that was over an hour ago. The policemen poked around downstairs and outside for a while, and a lot of nosy reporters came, but they've all gone now. And apparently, so has Greg."

"But he can't have gone far. Is his car gone?"

"No. That's just where he left it last night."

"And where are our cars — yours and mine?"

"They're here too. And so are Granddad's."

"Have you looked in Greg's room?"

"Yes. I've looked in all the rooms on this floor and downstairs."

"Then he must be just taking a walk."

"He's not on the grounds. I've looked everywhere for him."

"In the woods?"

"No. Why would he be in the woods?"

"He used to walk there."

"In the dead of the winter?"

"Sure."

His jaw tensed. "He's up to something. I don't trust him."

"Greg?"

"Yes, Greg."

"Oh, come now. Besides, what can he do now. The damage has already been done."

Bryan walked over and threw himself on the bed, letting his feet hang over the edge so his shoes wouldn't soil the counterpane. "God, I'm bushed!" he said, and closed his eyes. In a moment he was snoring gently.

I went out and closed the door quietly. Downstairs in the hall closet, I found a camel-colored coat sweater of Mr. Sedgwick's. I put it around my shoulders and went out. Greg must be somewhere around. Maybe if he saw me, he'd join me. I'd just pretend to be taking a walk.

As I went down the front porch steps, I heard a sound from one of the upstairs windows and looked up just in time to see a large flower pot rolling down the slightly slanting porch roof. I side-stepped just in time for it to miss my head. It crashed in several jagged pieces at my feet, the earth in the pot scattering over my blue satin evening slippers. The pot had contained an azalea plant which had a few pink flowers on it.

Where could it have come from? I backed away from the house and looked up, examining all the windows. They were all closed, the shades neatly pulled halfway down. And not a single window had a flower pot on its sill, either inside or outside.

I shuddered and pulled Mr. Sedgwick's voluminous sweater closer around me. Perhaps the falling of the azalea plant had been an accident? Maybe Agnes had put it out on the porch roof in the sun and then forgotten it? I'd ask her when I saw her.

But now I must try to find Greg. Going around the side of the house, I passed the windows to the library. I stopped for a moment and looked in. Everything was neat and tidy, and the room was empty. With a sigh I walked on, around to the back, past Greg's car standing in the circular driveway. By the license plate I could tell it was a rented car. Laying on the front seat was a pair of pigskin gloves. They had oil stains on them. I stood staring at them, feeling as if the ground had been pulled out from under my feet. What should I do? Should I take them and give them to the police? Or should I take them and confront Greg with them?

Then I began to rationalize. If they were gloves Greg had used to handle the pistol that was used to kill his grandfather, surely he wouldn't be careless enough or stupid enough to leave them there on the seat of his car for anyone to see. But they were gloves with oil on them!

On second thought, anyone could have put them there. Maybe they weren't even Greg's gloves. I opened the car door and picked them up. There was a silk label inside one of them. It had the name of a shop in Brazil. I rolled the gloves up, put them in the sweater pocket and closed the car door.

Now I definitely must find Greg. I would question him about them first. I couldn't — I simply couldn't take them to the police without his knowledge.

I walked on, my mind a seething mass of conflicting thoughts. John was in the garage washing the Cadillac, but apparently hadn't noticed me when I was standing by Greg's car. I said, "John, have you seen Mr. Greg?"

He looked up for a moment but didn't stop his work. "No, miss. He must be in the house. He didn't come back this way. He could have gone out the kitchen door, though, and I wouldn't have seen him."

I said, "If you see him, tell him I was looking for him."

John said, "Yes, miss. I will."

There was something about John that

held you off at arm's length. He was courteous, respectful, good at his job, but there was no warmth there. He was just the butler and handy man. On the other hand, you felt Agnes was your friend, as well as a servant in the house. You could talk to her, know that if you were in trouble she would help you in any way she could.

I wandered on in the crisp cold of the late morning. So Greg was in the house, was he? If he was, why couldn't Bryan have found him? Could he have accidentally pushed the azalea plant off the porch roof? My hand clenched around the gloves in the sweater pocket.

But of course Greg couldn't do anything like that. Not deliberately. And if he had done it accidentally, he'd have called to me and asked if I was all right, or rushed downstairs to see if I was hurt.

I wandered along through the back garden, frozen and barren, devoid of flowers, its bushes bare of leaves, then across the back lawn, brown and lumpy from frost. At the far side there was the footpath that led to the back driveway, and that in turn led to a lower road which went to the village. The woman or girl I'd seen from my window last night could have come this way and escaped by the same route.

At either side of the landscaped grounds was a wooded section that I knew belonged to Shadow Acres but which had been left wild and uncultivated to ensure privacy. The sun had burned away last night's fog and was shining through the bare, lacy branches of the trees, and the woods looked peaceful and inviting. I walked in a ways and then stopped to watch a squirrel skitter across my path and up a tree.

I listened to the soft, crackling noises one always hears in the woods. I wondered if Greg was in there anywhere. He liked to walk, and as a child and a young man, often went off by himself and walked either in this woods or the one on the opposite side of the estate. Often I'd walked with him. I listened carefully. If he was anywhere around, he'd be whistling. He always whistled when he walked by himself. But there were only the birds calling to one another, with a bluejay excitedly announcing to his feathered friends that there was an interloper in their private sanctuary.

I decided I'd go back and over to the other woods. Maybe Greg was over there.

I walked slowly through the mottled sunshine and had almost reached the lawn when something hit me in the back of the head.

Chapter Seven

For a couple of moments I was stunned and could only lean against a tree and press my hands to my head. I'd never had anything hurt so, and I had to press my hands hard to the injured place while tears of pain ran down my cheeks, and the bluejay shrieked frantically in a nearby tree.

I don't know how long I stood there, my forehead leaning against the tree trunk, but at last I was able to stand up straight and take my hands away from my head. When I did so, I saw they were smeared with blood.

"Oh dear!" I gasped, and experimentally felt of the injured place again. My hands came away with more blood on them, and now I could feel it trickling down the back of my neck.

I looked around. There was no one in sight, but at my feet was a sharp pointed stone, almost a rock. I picked it up and examined it. It had flecks of blood on it. My blood! And it was from Greg's rock collection. He'd been an enthusiastic geologist in his teens and had accumulated a very impressive and valuable collection of rocks from all over the world. Often I'd worked with him when he'd been labeling and cataloguing them, and I recognized this one, even though there was nothing on it to tell what it was. I knew it was a piece of bluestone, the kind that had been brought from Wales, centuries ago, to build Stonehenge, so the legend went. Greg had bought it from a boy in prep school who had traveled extensively and at the time wanted some quick cash. It was a rare specimen, and Greg had been very excited about getting it.

I remembered him telling me about Stonehenge. It is England's most important example of prehistoric architecture and is on Salisbury Plain, in Wiltshire, about eighty miles from London. We decided we'd like to see it some time.

But surely Greg wouldn't have shied one of his choice rocks at me! Was someone else trying to harm me and throw the blame on Greg?

I looked up in the trees, knowing full well the rock couldn't have fallen out of a tree. Nor had a bird thrown it at me. Not even an angry bluejay could do that.

Frightened now, I began to run, still holding the rock in my right hand. But I couldn't run very fast, because my knees felt weak and wouldn't work very well. So I was almost staggering when I reached the house and went into the kitchen.

Agnes was sitting at the kitchen table having a cup of coffee. When she saw me, she jumped up. "Miss Reda, what happened to you?" she cried.

I bowed my head and showed her. She touched my head gently. "Oh my!" she said. "Why, you're hurt! I'd better call the doctor."

I sank down in the chair she'd vacated, put the rock on the table, then covered my face with my hands. "Is it that bad?" I asked through my blood-smeared fingers. I was trembling now; hot one minute and cold the next.

"You've got a hole in your head. That's bad, isn't it?" She stamped out of the kitchen, and I heard her using the phone in the hall, calling Dr. Hanson, the Sedgwicks' family physician.

Just then Greg came in the back door. When he saw me he stopped; then he came quickly to me. "Chicken!" he said. "What happened to you?" He took my bloody hands in his and then, taking a handkerchief from his pocket, wiped my face. "You've smeared your face," he said gently. "What happened?"

91

I showed him my head. "My God!" he cried. "Who did that you?"

"I don't know. Where were *you?*"

"Over in the woods."

My heart sank. "Which woods?"

"The one on the other side of the garage."

I looked up at him. "You're sure?"

"Of course I'm sure."

"John said he hadn't seen you."

"He was back in the garage when I passed, and I didn't feel like talking to him, so I didn't call attention to myself."

I said, "Oh."

Then he asked, "Where were *you?*"

"In the other woods. Somebody threw this rock at me." I pushed the rock toward him.

He picked it up and looked at it. Then he looked at me. "It's from my rock collection," he said. "It's my Stonehenge bluestone. There's nothing like it around here."

"I know," I said, holding his gaze. "I recognized it."

He was holding it on the open palm of his hand. "That's strange," he said, a muscle beginning to throb in his temple.

"Yes, it is."

He gave me a quick, inquiring look. "You don't think I — ?"

"If you did, it would have been very

stupid. But the chances were in your favor. It was a thousand to one I'd ever know what hit me. And anyone examining the spot, even if they found this stone, wouldn't recognize it as Stonehenge bluestone unless he was a geologist. And I don't believe policemen are."

He put the stone in the side pocket of his jacket, ignoring my insinuation. "Did you see or hear anyone?" he asked me.

I started to shake my head, but it hurt too much, so I just said, "No. There wasn't anyone around. It was like the azalea plant falling off the porch roof when I went out — and just missing my head."

"When did that happen?" Greg demanded.

"A little while ago, as I was going out for a walk. I went out the front door, and just as I reached the bottom of the porch steps an azalea came crashing off the porch roof and just missed my head."

"An azalea plant?" Agnes asked, coming back into the kitchen. "*My* azalea plant?"

I looked over at her. "Do you have an azalea plant?" I asked her.

"Sure I have an azalea plant. It's on the table in our sitting room. It's been there since last summer."

I sighed. "Well, it isn't there now. It's

on the front walk, smashed!"

Agnes stared at me. "It can't be!"

"Go and look."

With a skeptical expression on her face, she hurried up the back stairs. Greg called, "Bring some clean cloths for Reda's head."

When she'd gone, I took the gloves from the sweater pocket and gave them to him. "Here, hide these. Quick! And when you can, burn them."

He took them and looked down at the ball into which I'd rolled them. "What is it?" he asked.

"Your gloves. They were on the front seat of your car, in full view. And they have oil on them!"

He stared at them for a moment, then began to chuckle.

"What's so funny?" I asked.

He looked up at me. "You! You precious babe in the woods." Then he sobered. "But why don't you give them to the police? They are the evidence you needed, aren't they, to clear Bryan?"

I couldn't answer that for a moment. Then I said crossly, "Don't be a fool! Hide them. Quick! Before Agnes comes back. And burn them, for heaven sakes!"

He looked at the gloves for a moment, then put them in his pocket, on top of the piece of bluestone. Then he went to work on my head, getting a clean napkin and soaking it with cold water, then holding the water-soaked cloth to the wound to try to stop the bleeding. His hands were gentle, and he worked with an efficiency that inspired confidence. Could he, I wondered, have thrown the rock at me? It seemed unbelievable. But how would anyone else have had a rock from his boyhood collection?

I asked, "Is your rock collection here, Greg?"

"The last I saw of it, it was."

"When did you see it last?"

"The summer before I went away to college. I was here for a month and I brought it with me. When I left, I asked Granddad to keep it for me."

"And did he tell you where he was going to put it?"

"Yes. He gave it to John and told him to find a safe place for it, and John put it in one of the bookcase cupboards in the library."

"Then anyone could get at it, unless the cupboard was kept locked?"

"I don't remember any of the cupboards having keys. They never went in much for keys around here."

"Maybe you'd better go see if you can find the collection?" I suggested.

"Good idea. Here; hold this cloth tight to your head for a minute."

I took the cloth and did as he said, and he rushed out of the kitchen. In a couple of minutes he was back, his face white and tense. "It's there, but the rock that hit you is missing."

We looked at one another without speaking, both with apprehension filling our hearts. Finally I said, "And you didn't take it?"

He exploded then. "Of course I didn't take it!" he yelled at me. "Stop being so accusing. If I wanted to get rid of you, I'd shoot you, or something more final than throwing a rock at you."

"Like you did your grandfather?"

He clenched his hands, and his jaw tightened. *"Et tu, Brute?"* he said, giving me a look that tore at my heart. It was the last straw, and I put my head down on my crossed arms on the table and began to cry.

He let me cry for a moment, then sank down on his knees beside me and put his arms around me. "I'm sorry," I sobbed. "I didn't mean that."

His lips against my cheek, he said, "I know you didn't, chicken."

Agnes found us that way when she came running down the stairs. "It's gone!" she said in a scared-sounding voice.

I raised my head. Greg got to his feet, and she gave him some clean towels and a box of sterile gauze.

"Look on the front walk," I said, beginning to sniffle but sitting perfectly still so Greg could work on my aching head.

Agnes hurried to the front of the house and opened the door. I could hear her stamp across the wooden porch. In a couple of minutes she returned. "There's nothing out there," she announced. "And the walk has been hosed off." She thought a moment, then added, "If John saw it, he must have cleaned it up."

"John?" I asked.

"You don't think my John threw the azalea plant at you?" Agnes asked in amazement. "He's been out back ever since breakfast."

Greg and I exchanged glances. "Well, somebody did," I said wearily. "And someone threw this rock at me." I began to cry silently. "Somebody is trying to kill me!" I said raggedly.

Greg dropped on his knees beside me again and took me into his arms. "Poor little chicken," he said. "Why would anyone want to kill *you?*"

"I don't know," I said, laying my aching

head on his broad shoulder. Maybe he was the one who had tried to murder me, but somehow I just couldn't feel afraid of him. I said, "Greg, I'm scared."

After soothing me for a few minutes, Greg asked Agnes, "What did the doctor say? You did get him on the phone?"

"Dr. Hanson, yes. He said he'd be right out. Said it sounded like she'd need some stitches, and she'd better go to the hospital and have X-rays."

Greg's arms tightened around me, and neither he nor Agnes nor I heard Bryan come into the room until he yanked Greg away from me and swung at his jaw. "I told you to leave her alone!" he told Greg viciously.

Instantly Greg was on his feet. There was a cracking sound, and the next thing I knew Bryan was on the floor with a dazed look on his face, and he was holding onto his jaw.

Greg stood looking down at him for a moment, then helped him to his feet. Quietly he said, "Let's stop playing games, Bryan. We have something worse to worry about now than each other."

Chapter Eight

When Dr. Hanson arrived, he complimented Greg on his first aid job and said he didn't think the wound was serious. "Just a scalp wound," he said. "They bleed a lot but don't do any serious damage."

He suggested we go up to my room near a bathroom, and Agnes helped me up the stairs. He thought Greg and Bryan had better stay downstairs.

When Dr. Hanson had finished with me, he suggested I go to bed and stay there for a couple of days.

"But I can't," I protested. "Tomorrow is the inquest. I have to go to that."

Putting his things into his bag, he said, "Um. So you do. And I'll have to go, too. But you can at least go to bed now and stay there until tomorrow." He clicked the bag shut and straightened. He was short and fat, with thinning white hair and kindly blue eyes. "Are you going to notify the police about this?" He motioned to my head.

"I hadn't thought about it," I said, quickly imagining what the police would make of the fact that I'd been hit by a stone from Greg's collection. But he had the stone in his pocket, and I didn't have to tell them it belonged to Greg. "Do you think I should tell the police?" I asked.

"I think it would be a good idea. We don't want anything more to happen around here."

After he left, Agnes helped me into bed, getting me one of her nightdresses so I wouldn't have to sleep in my bra and briefs again. I was surprised to see how pretty the nightdress was. It was a pale blue sheer nylon with straps of lace over the shoulders and a narrow bow of ribbon at the front of the scooped out and lace-edged neck. There was also lace at the bottom, which was only knee length. I tried to imagine Agnes wearing it but couldn't. "Why, Agnes," I said, "this is lovely."

She grunted. "It's Christine's," she said. "My daughter. She left it here the last time she visited us."

"Christine? I didn't know you had a daughter, Agnes."

"Not many people did — or do. We didn't want her to grow up in servitude, the way we had."

"But where did she live?"

"At first she lived with my sister who had

married a plumber. He made good money, and they had a nice apartment in the Bronx, and Christine went to school down there."

"But didn't you see her?"

"Oh yes, we used to go down on our days off. But she got so she didn't pay much attention to us. She thought more of my sister and her husband than she did of John and me."

"But that's awful!" I cried.

She shrugged. "You get so you accept those things," she said. "It was better than having her grow up here, as the daughter of the servants."

"But, Agnes, people wouldn't have thought of her that way. Why, nobody thinks of you and John that way. You're practically part of the family."

She picked up my bra and briefs, saying, "I'll wash these for you."

I said, "Thank you." Then, noticing there was considerable blood on the dress she'd lent me, I said, "I'm sorry about your dress. I'll get you a new one."

But she tut-tutted and said, "That won't be necessary. Besides, I'll wash and iron it so it will be all ready for you to wear again in the morning. Cold water will take out the bloodstains." She went over to the center of the three windows which formed the bay

101

and opened it a few inches. "Need a little air in here if you're going to sleep," she said.

Just as she reached the door, I asked, "Agnes, where is your daughter now?"

She turned, and I thought there was a look of defiance in her dark eyes. "She has a job down in the city. She's a — what you call a 'bunny' in a cocktail lounge," she said. "And she has her own apartment now."

"But you see her more often now that she's grown up?"

"Yes. She comes up here now and spends her days off sometimes and stays all night. Mr. Sedgwick said he didn't mind."

"I'm sure he didn't. How old is she?"

"Same age as you." She started to go out.

"I'd like to meet her sometime," I said, and meant it.

"You probably will," she told me, and went out, closing the door quietly behind her.

The doctor had given me a sedative, and after Agnes left me I dropped off to sleep. When I awoke it was late afternoon and everything was quiet. My head ached, but otherwise I felt all right. The room seemed warm, and I threw off part of the bedcovers. I wondered where everybody was. There was a tapestry bell-pull hanging over the bedside table which I knew connected with the kitchen. But I didn't want to disturb

Agnes when I didn't actually need anything.

I hadn't had any lunch and was a little hungry, but the clock on the fireplace mantel was pointing to four, so in a couple of hours it would be dinner time. But I would have loved a cup of tea right that very minute.

I reached over and pulled the tapestry band that made the bell ring down in the kitchen. But it got me nowhere.

I waited fifteen minutes. Then I pulled the band again. Still nothing. Then I heard footsteps overhead. Agnes must be up in her room. Perhaps she rested for a while at this time of day. And she always changed from her daytime uniform of blue to a black one for dinner. At least she had when Mr. Sedgwick was alive. Now there was no telling what she would do.

The daylight was growing dimmer, and I closed my eyes. I still was a little sleepy from the sedative. I began to think about the house of Shadow Acres. As I've said before, I'd spent many pleasant hours there — and also some not so pleasant.

I began to wonder about Bryan's father. Could what Agnes told me be true? And had his wife, Sybil, known about his extracurricular activities? Had Bryan known? Had he remembered that Sunday afternoon when he'd had chicken pox more vividly than I had? If he had, he had never mentioned it to me.

I wondered if Bryan had known about Christine Johnson or had ever seen her. Had Greg? Strange I'd never heard about her when we were all growing up.

And what about Greg's mother and father? Had the whispered gossip about his mother been true? Or had she just kicked over the traces because she couldn't stand the perfection of the Sedgwick family? Had her husband felt badly about the divorce? Or had he been glad to get rid of her? I wondered if Greg had known any of the details.

As kids and growing young people, we — Bryan, Greg and I — had been to engrossed with our own affairs to give much, if any thought to our elders, other than to accept from them the love and care they gave us. I guess all parents and peripheral relatives are taken for granted by children. It's next to impossible for young people to think of the previous generation as having the same kind of feelings they themselves have.

I decided to have a talk with both Bryan and Greg about it at the first opportunity, and then I dozed off.

People were shouting outside and inside the house, and as I gradually began to pull myself awake, I started to cough. My nose and throat felt uncomfortable, and my left hand and arm were hurting.

I opened my eyes and sat up in bed, choking and gagging, and then I saw my room was filled with smoke and one side of the bed was on fire.

I began to scream and jumped out of bed. I stumbled to the door, but it wouldn't open and there wasn't any key. How had it gotten locked? I wondered.

Someone was pounding on the other side of the door, and I heard Bryan shouting, "Reda! Open the door! Let us in!"

"I can't!" I screamed. But I didn't have much voice left to scream with.

I turned and ran to a window, only to discover it was closed, and I couldn't open it either. Then I saw it was locked. All three windows were closed and the catch was turned. A man's head appeared over the porch roof. It was Greg, who had climbed up on a ladder. Just as he was coming across the roof to my window, the fire engine came screaming along the road and into the driveway. It stopped, and firemen jumped off and ran toward the house with ladders, pickaxes, hand fire extinguishers and the various things they bring with them.

Greg, seeing me at the window, called,

"Open the window! Quick!"

With shaking hands I turned the catch, and together we got the sash open.

"Climb out!" Greg told me. But by that time the room was so full of smoke and I'd inhaled so much of it I could feel myself slipping into unconsciousness.

Then I felt strong arms lifting me, and cold air blew across my face. That was all I remembered.

The next thing I knew a man's voice was saying, "Chicken, it's Greg. Open your eyes darling." I tried to take a breath and found that I could, but my eyes and throat, nose and lungs smarted.

With a great effort I managed to get my eyes opened and discovered I was in bed in a strange room, and an oxygen tent was around me. On one side of the bed was a man in a white hospital coat and a nurse. At the foot of the bed was a policeman, and on the other side of the bed was Greg, looking disheveled and exhausted, his face streaked with black soot and the edges of his hair singed. When my eyes met his, he smiled, and I realized he had his head sticking through a side opening of the oxygen tent and was holding my hand. My other hand and arm were swathed in bandages.

I tried to smile but couldn't. As a matter

of fact, I didn't feel much like moving any part of me.

The doctor said something to the nurse, and she began taking the oxygen tent away. When I was clear of it, the doctor asked, "How do you feel?"

"I don't know," I said, scarcely above a whisper. "I feel queer."

He smiled. "And no wonder. You nearly killed yourself."

"Oh, no!" I said. "No!"

I felt Greg's hand tighten on mine, and it seemed to give me strength enough to come back to life.

The policeman came around to the side of the bed. The doctor said, "She's not well enough to be questioned yet."

The policeman looked annoyed. "I have to make a report." He turned to Greg. "Does she usually smoke in bed?" he asked him.

Greg looked questioningly at me. "Do you chicken?" he asked.

I said, "No, of course not. I don't smoke ever — anywhere."

"But there was a cigarette found in your bed. That's what started the fire. You must have fallen asleep while you were smoking. It happens every day."

I tried to sit up, but was too weak, so I had

to lie back again. "But I don't smoke, I tell you! I don't like it."

The policeman shrugged, and the doctor said, "Don't question her any more. She needs rest," and adroitly maneuvered him out of the room. The nurse motioned Greg to leave, too, but he said, "Can't I sit with her for a while? I won't upset her."

"Please let him," I pleaded.

The nurse said, "Well, for a few minutes. But she ought to sleep. We'll be putting her into the oxygen tent again in a little while."

She went out of the room, and Greg pulled a chair over to the bed and sat down, taking hold of my hand. "Try to sleep," he said gently. "I'll stay here beside you."

I turned my head away, not wanting him to see my face all screwed up and blotchy with the tears I couldn't keep back. "Somebody is trying to kill me," I sobbed. "I wasn't smoking. You know I don't."

"I know you didn't used to. But you could have taken it up while I was away."

"No, I didn't. You never wanted me to. Remember?"

His hand tightened around mine. "Yes, I remember."

"Well, I never have."

He leaned over and wiped away my tears with the corner of the bed sheet and turned my head so I had to look at him. Then he leaned over and touched his lips to mine.

I closed my eyes and tried to deny the little thrill that went through me; then I asked, "Where's Bryan?"

I opened my eyes just in time to see his lips tighten. "I guess he's still back at the house," he said. "They rushed you here in an ambulance, and I rode along with you. I didn't see Bryan anywhere around."

I tried to remember back to the moment when I had awakened and discovered my bed was afire. "He was out in the hall," I said, "hammering on the door. But it was locked, and I couldn't open it."

"Had you locked it?"

"No. And I don't remember seeing a key for it."

I began to cough, and the nurse came in. "You'd better go now," she told Greg. "I'm going to give her a sedative; then I'll put her in the oxygen tent for a while. It will ease her breathing." She smiled at me. "We'll have you all right in a couple of days," she said.

I'd forgotten about my head, but all of a sudden it began to ache. Greg bent down and kissed my cheek. "I'll be seeing you," he promised.

As he was going out the door, I heard him say to the nurse, "She'd better have police protection as long as she's here."

The nurse nodded and closed the door, then began to be very efficient around my bed.

I realized for the first time that I was wearing a hospital gown, and my mind flew back to Agnes bringing me her daughter's blue nylon gown. I said, "Oh dear!"

The nurse said, "What's the matter?"

"My nightdress," I said. "When I was rescued, all I had on was a short, low-necked and very sheer nightdress and — that's all!"

The nurse laughed. "Think nothing of it. You looked charming, except for some smoke smudges and singeing."

"You mean —"

She winked at me and brought me a pill and a glass of water. "I mean, if he carried you down a ladder in that wisp of blue and didn't fall in love with you, he's no man."

"Oh, no!" I gasped, and covered my face with my free hand. But she took it away gently and said, "Stop the dramatics and take this pill. And if you don't want him, I'll take him. Any day."

I swallowed the pill and took a few sips of water. When I'd finished I gulped, "But you don't understand. I'm engaged to someone else: his cousin."

The nurse took the glass. "What happened to your head?" she asked, changing the subject.

I sighed. "Someone threw a rock at me."

She looked at me skeptically but didn't say anything; just began putting the oxygen tent around me again.

Chapter Nine

Bryan came to see me in the morning. He looked as if he hadn't much sleep. It was ten o'clock, and I was sitting up in bed. I'd had my breakfast, and the nurse had bathed me and combed my hair. I didn't have on any makeup, but I didn't seem to care. The nurse had told me I looked fine, and I was willing to believe her.

I held out my unbandaged hand to Bryan, and he took it and leaned down and kissed me. "I'm sorry I couldn't get here last night," he said, "but I —" He let go of my hand, brought a chair over from the other side of the room and sat down beside the bed. "I guess I had a drop too much after the firemen left and —"

"I understand," I said, not wanting to hear the rest of it. I tried to smile but only succeeded in stretching my lips a little. I said, "Someone put a lighted cigarette in my bed and locked me in."

He stared at me. "That's crazy!" he said.

"It's true. Someone at Shadow Acres is trying to kill me, Bryan."

He took my hand and gripped it tightly. "That's ridiculous. Why would anyone want to kill you?"

I sighed. "Why did someone kill your grandfather?"

He let go of my hand. "That was different."

"How different?"

He shrugged. "How should I know?"

"*You* didn't kill him, did you, Bryan?"

His eyes opened wide in surprise. "You don't think that, do you?"

"No. No, I don't. But somebody did kill him."

He leaned over closer to me. "Who else but Greg?" he said. "He had a motive. Granddad made him go away after —"

I flounced on the bed, and my head started aching. "Don't be silly! Greg wouldn't kill anybody for any reason, least of all his grandfather. And no one will ever convince me he would or did."

Bryan leaned back in his chair. He was wearing a pair of slacks that must have been his grandfather's and that fitted him the way Agnes' dress had fit me. His face was very white. "You're still in love with him, aren't you?" he said.

I tensed, and my heart began to pound. "No! Of course I'm not! How could I be afraid after what he did?"

He turned his head away from me and gazed out the window. There was nothing to see but gray sky, but it held his gaze. "You don't love me, Reda. You never have," he said, a bitter twist to his mouth. "It's been Greg with you ever since we were kids."

"It used to be."

He shook his head, and his gaze left the gray sky and returned to my face. "No," he said. "You've been putting on a good act. But when Greg has his arms around you, you're a different girl from the one you are when I have my arms around you."

I felt tears flood my eyes and couldn't speak either to affirm or deny the truth of his words.

The nurse came in with a box of flowers. "Present for you," she said with her professional cheerfulness, put the box on the bed beside me and left the room.

I looked at Bryan. "From you?"

He shook his head. "I'm afraid I never even thought of it."

My hand shook as I pulled off the ribbon tape from the box and lifted the lid. Opening the green waxed tissue, I saw a dozen red roses. They were lovely. I picked up the small white envelope that was tucked among them and drew out the card. On it was written:

"To the only girl in the world. Now, before and forever.

Greg."

Tears began to roll down my cheeks, and I let the card drop back among the flowers. Bryan reached over and picked it up, read it, and with an angry, explosive sound threw it back at the roses. He jumped to his feet. "That does it!" he cried, and stalked out of the room.

When the nurse came in a few minutes later, I had the roses in my good arm, my lips to one of them, and my flesh was completely unconscious of the thorns pricking it.

Greg came to see me after lunch. He said, "I knew Bryan was coming this morning, so I waited. And incidentally, the inquest has been put off until Monday because of your accident." He took my hand and held it with both of his, but he didn't kiss me. His touch sent a warm, tingling feeling up my arm and gave warmth to my heart. I said, "Thanks for the roses. They're lovely." The nurse had put them in a glass vase, and they were on the dresser so I could easily see and enjoy them.

He smiled and squeezed my hand. "I meant what I said on the card."

I could feel a quick blush burning my face and neck. "You mustn't feel that way about me," I said, my voice catching in my throat. "It's too late." I pulled away my hand, and he sat down in the chair beside the bed.

"Sure about that?" he asked, a quizzical look in his eyes.

I worried the sheet with my unbandaged hand. "Yes. I'm marrying Bryan next week. The invitations have all been sent out."

"Don't do it, Reda. You'll regret it."

I shook my head. "No, I won't. I love Bryan, and I'm sure we'll make a go of it."

"And I'm sure you won't."

My eyes reluctantly met his. "Why do you say that?"

"Because to begin with, you're still in love with me, just as I'm in love with you. And in addition to that, I know Bryan. He wouldn't make you happy."

"You don't know anything about it. Bryan and I have been very happy, since you've been away."

Two lines appeared in his forehead as his brows drew together in a frown. "How much time have you spent alone with him?"

"That's a strange question."

"Perhaps I'd better clarify it. What I'm getting at is — have you spent much time alone together, without other people

116

around? Or have you always been in a crowd, with another couple — not just alone, you two?"

His probing question surprised me, and for the first time I realized Bryan and I hadn't spent much time alone together. He was always too restless to spend an evening alone just with me. He always arranged for us to be going somewhere, doing something with other people. Take Wednesday evening. As I thought about it, I wasn't conscious of the fact that Greg's eyes were holding mine. When I realized it, I felt embarrassed and looked quickly away, toward his roses. I began remembering all the times he and I had spent together — alone. For hours we'd walked in the woods at Shadow Acres, hand in hand, sometimes talking, sometimes being silent. We'd spent hours together, studying, talking about life, books, everything. We'd spent hours reading, each with his own book, but content to be in the same room. To sum it up: just being together had been enough for us always. It had never been that way with Bryan and me. But I couldn't and wouldn't admit that to Greg. Never, never, never!

I said, "Greg, how much do you know about our parents — yours and mine and Bryan's?"

His eyebrows raised questioningly. "Why do you ask that?"

"Because Agnes said something yesterday that made me begin to wonder."

"What did she say?"

"I'd rather not repeat it."

"About *my* parents, yours or Bryan's?"

"I'd rather not specify." Then I added, "Well, how much do you know about yours?"

He looked at me thoughtfully for a long time before he said, "I know all about them, and they're swell people. They are down in South America, and my mother and father are remarried."

I sat up straight, crying, "Oh! How wonderful! But what about the other man?"

"Dane Holcolm?"

"I'd forgotten his name. As I remember it, he was her leading man."

He smiled ruefully. "Dad was her only leading man — and always will be. Dane just happened to be a convenience for a while, like Bryan has been for you."

I sank back on my pillow. "I'm glad your mother and father are together again. But you're wrong about Bryan and me."

He leaned over and patted my arm. "Am I, chicken?" he asked. "I don't think so. And I'll tell you why, show you why." He got up, took my face gently in his two strong hands and pressed his lips to mine, firmly yet softly. I felt myself draw in a deep, quivering breath as the thrill of his touch took possession of me and my lips parted beneath his. The next thing I knew, my uninjured arm was around his neck and I was holding him as close to me as I could. Time seemed to stop, and I closed my eyes and let the ecstasy of his touch enfold me.

After a long time he gently pulled away and took his lips from mine. His eyes had moisture in them and glistened like stars as he straightened up. Huskily he said, "That's why!" and left the room.

Chapter Ten

After Greg had left and I had my emotions under control once more, I tried to remember things about my childhood — our childhood — Greg's, Bryan's and mine. Why Natalie Sedgwick left her husband, divorced him and married her leading man.

As I remembered Natalie, she was a sweet and very pretty woman. And as far as I could tell, being a child at the time, she and her husband were very much in love. I remembered the exchanged glances, loaded with love and admiration, that used to pass between them, the touching of hands.

I also remembered the whispered innuendoes about her. She was a flirt, they said, *they* being the rest of the family. My own mother and father always defended her. "She's so beautiful," my mother said once, "she can't help attracting men."

"She can help encouraging them," Sybil Sedgwick snapped.

"I'm sure she doesn't mean anything by it," my mother said. "She's an actress, and it is second nature to her to try to attract attention to herself. Sort of a stock in trade."

"Nonsense!" Mrs. Sedgwick, Senior, said. "She's a typical siren, that's what's the matter with her." Then she added, "Mind you, I like her; I like her very much. You can't help but like her. But I just don't think she is the right wife for my son."

At the time, naturally, I didn't know what she meant. But now, as I thought about it, I could understand. Natalie, titian-haired, tall and stately, with green-gray eyes, smooth, creamy skin and a beautiful figure, had only to enter a room and men caught their breath. Instantly she was the center of attraction, whether she wanted to be or not. And as I remember it, her husband, Greg's father, used to get a kick out of it. Often he would just stay in the background and watch with an enigmatic little smile on his handsome face.

Though he wouldn't admit it, I think even old Mr. Sedgwick was taken by her and felt his pulses quicken when she entered a room, even though he didn't approve of her because she was an actress.

Naturally, her hours were irregular. When she was in a show, she never got home to Greenwich until midnight or after, and on matinee days she would have to leave before noon.

Then there was the problem of her husband's irregular hours as a newspaperman. With the demands on his time, he was not able to squire around his successful and beautiful actress wife. This left her alone when she needed an escort, as she often did. So what could she do but accept the attentions of other men — her leading men, playboys about town, anyone who was free to escort her to parties, places like Sardi's, night clubs, etc., where she had to go to be seen? It was therefore inevitable that she and her husband should drift apart, even though they dearly loved each other.

This left Greg (my Greg) often alone with servants. I guess that was why he and I saw so much of each other. Our houses were within walking distance, and on the way home from school Greg often stopped at our place, where he knew he'd receive a warm welcome from my mother and me. An after-school snack was always available, and often he would stay on for dinner and we'd do our lessons together.

I remember the incident that triggered his mother's and father's break-up. It was Thanksgiving, and we had all been invited to dinner at Shadow Acres. Greg's father was able to be there, but his mother had to play a matinee as well as an evening performance.

During dinner she was mentioned several times — derogatorily. Old Mrs. Sedgwick, who was otherwise a darling, said, "It's too bad Natalie isn't here."

Her son, Gregory, didn't answer.

Then Robert said, "I think you're a fool to put up with it, Greg. You make enough money. She doesn't have to work. Why don't you put your foot down?"

Gregory swallowed a piece of turkey. "Because she'd be miserable being just a housewife."

"Then why on earth did you marry her?" Robert asked.

"Because I loved her. And I still love her. And I wish you'd all mind your own business!"

Grace Sedgwick said gently, "But it's not good for your boy. He needs his mother. As it is, he scarcely sees her."

"I do too!" young Greg cried. "I see her almost every day."

Grace Sedgwick, his grandmother, smiled at him benignly. "But not for very long periods, I'm afraid."

Young Greg looked at his father. "We do, too, don't we, Dad? We see her plenty, and we like it that way!"

"Like seeing your mother only for snatches at a time?" Sybil asked with raised eyebrows. "Why, you poor child. You don't know what it is to have a mother — a real mother."

Greg threw his knife and fork down on his plate with a bang and jumped to his feet, overthrowing his chair, which made another bang. "You shut up!" he cried. "I'd rather have *my* mother *part* of the time than *you all* the time. You make me sick! I've seen Uncle Robert making up to my mother, so *you* needn't talk. He's just as bad as the rest of the men!" With that he gave his fallen chair a kick and ran out of the room.

His father called, "Greg! Come back here!" But the boy was out in the hall on his way to the front door. "I won't!" he cried. "I hate them all!" In another moment there was the bang of the front door, and he was gone.

His father sighed and put his knife and fork on his plate, carefully and quietly. With another deep sigh he said, "I'm sorry. I'm sure he didn't mean to be rude."

His father cleared his throat. "You have a problem, son. Perhaps it's time you did something about it."

His son looked at him. "Such as what?"

His father stood up and began to carve more turkey, and I remember how impressive he looked, there at the end of the beautifully appointed table. "Such as having a talk with Natalie," he said quietly.

"But what good would that do? I can't ask her to give up her career. It's her life!"

"Her life should be her son and her husband," his mother said gently. "A woman's place is in the home."

Gregory crumpled his napkin in his fist and threw it angrily on the table. "Oh, bosh!" he cried. "How old-fashioned can you get?"

"It's not a case of fashion, old or new," Sybil said. "It's a case of common sense."

Greg glared down at her. "You keep out of it!" he told her. "And my advice to you is — clean up your own house before you try to clean up mine!" He turned to his mother, then his father. "Please excuse me," he said. "I think I'd better go after Greg."

His mother said, "Tell him we are going to have plum pudding and hard sauce for dessert."

"What he needs is a good strapping, not dessert," Robert said. But his brother didn't answer him; he merely turned and walked out of the house, and neither he nor his son returned that day.

I heard later that they had driven into the city. First they'd seen the evening performance of Natalie's play; then they'd all had something to eat at Sardi's before driving back home, and when they reached home they had had it out. The constant nagging from the family had had its effect even on strong-minded Gregory Sedgwick. As they say, a drop of water at a time can wear away a stone, if it is kept up long enough. So that night Gregory asked Natalie to give up her career, and she flatly refused. She had said if he didn't want her, just as she was, then there were others who did, particularly Dane Holcolm. And that did it.

For a while after that I didn't see much of Greg. He even avoided me and my mother. It made me feel badly, but my mother said, "Let him alone. He'll come around again after a while."

His father was seldom home after the divorce, and after a while he sold their house and moved into the city, and Greg went away to school. His father spent a lot of time out of the country on foreign assignments, and I didn't see him at all after he left Greenwich.

Chapter Eleven

The nurse got me up later that afternoon for a while, and then not again until after lunch the next day, which was Sunday. Bryan, Greg and Agnes came to see me in the afternoon, all together, so what little conversation there was, was impersonal. It was arranged that Agnes and Bryan would come together the next day to take me to the inquest. Greg looked tense and very annoyed, but he didn't say anything.

So Monday afternoon I left the hospital in the care of Bryan and Agnes, as had been arranged. Greg, John and Dr. Hanson were to meet us at the courthouse.

Agnes brought my clothes, the only ones I had to wear. She'd washed and ironed her dress for me, and the bloodstains were completely gone. She'd also laundered my briefs, bra and stockings. My mink cape reeked of smoke, and Agnes apologized as if it were her fault. "I've had it hanging out in the air all morning," she said, "but you just can't get that smoke smell out once it gets in."

I said, "Don't worry about it. I'll have the

furrier clean it as soon as I get back to the city."

I was only too glad to get out of the hospital gown, get some kind of street clothes on and get out of the hospital. I felt weak but otherwise all right, although I looked as if I'd been through the wars, with the patch bandage on my head, and my left arm and hand swathed in bandages. They'd X-rayed my head at the hospital and found it was all right — just a scalp wound, as Dr. Hanson had thought.

I'd dreaded the inquest, but it really didn't amount to much. The coroner read his report, which stated Mr. Gregory, Senior, had been shot with a .32 caliber Smith & Wesson pistol, recently oiled, identified as belonging to the deceased. The slug had been taken from his head and matched those left in the pistol. He'd been dead about an hour before the coroner had arrived at the scene, which put the time just a few minutes before I had arrived.

We were all questioned, but nothing new was evolved. I avoided telling that Bryan had met me at the door to the library with the gun in his hand. I also avoided mentioning the girl or woman I had seen from my window later that night. Nor did I tell of the meeting and argument Greg and Bryan had had in their grandfather's library at three o'clock in the morning. And there was no reason to tell about the stone that had hit me while I was walking in the woods, or the azalea plant that had just missed my head. Agnes had brought me a silk scarf to put around my head so the patch on the back wouldn't show.

I realized that at the actual trial, if anyone was ultimately accused of the murder, all these things might be squeezed from me. But for the time being my secrets were safe, and the verdict of the inquest was that Mr. Sedgwick had either committed suicide or been killed by an unknown person.

However, I was well enough versed in the procedure of the law to know that the inquest wasn't going to be the end of it. Hadn't my own father been a lawyer? And I'd heard him talk about "the long arm of the law."

Bryan and I rode back to Shadow Acres in his car, and Agnes, John and Greg went in the station wagon, with John driving.

As soon as we reached Shadow Acres and had all gotten out in the driveway, Agnes said, "I'll bring tea into the living room in a few minutes, if anyone's interested. John will make a fire in the fireplace."

"I could use a drink," Bryan said.

Greg said, "Tea will be fine, Agnes, and maybe some of your famous cup cakes?"

She smiled. "No cup cakes, but there's part of a chocolate layer cake."

"Splendid!" Greg said. "How about you, Reda?"

"Fine," I said, not able to meet his eyes because I suddenly remembered the many chocolate layer cakes we had consumed together when we were children. Some Agnes had baked and some my mother had made for us.

John drove the station wagon into the garage, after leaving us all out in the driveway, and Bryan, leaving his car in the driveway, followed Greg, Agnes and me in through the back door that led into the center hall.

Bryan immediately headed for the liquor tray in the dining room, and Greg sauntered toward the living room to wait for tea and chocolate cake.

Before I went upstairs to my room to freshen up, I said to Agnes, "By the way, Friday afternoon, when I was resting in my room, about four o'clock, before the fire, I rang for you. I wanted some tea. But I guess you were up in your room, because there was no answer to my ring."

She looked at me in surprise. "No," she said, "I wasn't upstairs at all after the time I went up to see about the azalea. I might have been down in the cellar getting some things from the freezer for dinner. But I wasn't up in my room."

I watched her face and decided she was telling the truth. "That's strange," I said. "I was sure I heard footsteps up there. Maybe it was John."

Quickly she said, "No. It wasn't him either. He was outside all afternoon." She dropped her hat and coat on a chair and began bustling around getting the tea things ready.

I said, "Does that room I was in have a key?"

"It may have. I have a big bunch of keys up in my room."

I walked slowly out to the hall. I was sure I'd heard footsteps overhead on Friday afternoon. If it hadn't been either Agnes or John, who had it been? It had sounded like a woman's footsteps. Could it have been Christine? But no. If she had a job in the city and only visited her parents occasionally, it wouldn't have been she.

I'd almost reached the front stairs when Agnes called me. "Oh, Miss Reda, I forgot. Your room was so damaged by fire and smoke, you'll have to use one of the rooms on the other side of the house. I've moved your things over to the room across the hall from the boys."

I said, "Oh, all right. Only I didn't have anything to move, really."

As I went up the long flight of stairs, I realized how weak I was. Halfway up, my knees gave out and I had to sit down on the steps. Greg, who had evidently been pacing around the living room, came to the door and saw me. He was up the stairs in nothing flat. "Chicken, what's the matter?" he asked, reaching for me.

I managed a smile. "It's my knees. They seem to have turned to tissue paper," I explained.

Without a word he picked me up and carried me to the second floor. As we reached the top step, I told him about Agnes moving me to the room opposite his. He said, "Yes, I guess that other room is rather a mess."

When he had deposited me on the bed in the smaller room, he said, "Suppose I bring your tea up to you?" But I said, "No, thanks just the same. I'd rather have it downstairs with you and Bryan. I'll just wash up a bit, and then I'll come down."

He strolled over to a window. "I'll wait for you," he said. "Give you a piggyback down."

I laughed. "I'm afraid I'm too big for that."

"Then we'll do it straight," he said, "the way I brought you up." He grinned at me, and my heart wobbled.

The room was similar to the one I'd been in before; only this one was pink and ivory, the bathroom all white with pink towels. And it was at the front of the house, instead of the back, so I couldn't see the back gardens. The four posts of the bed were free of a canopy, and there was a dresser instead of a highboy.

Greg waited for me until I came out of the bathroom, my face and hands clean, my hair neatly combed.

"Atta girl," he said, and came and picked me up as easily as if I were a child. Quite naturally I put my arms around his neck and let my cheek rest against his as he carried me out of the room and down the stairs.

Luckily, Bryan wasn't in sight, or he would surely have made a row if he'd seen me in Greg's arms.

John came in and made a fire in the fireplace, and soon after Agnes brought tea, watercress and cucumber sandwiches and chocolate layer cake. I asked, "Have you seen Bryan?" and she said, "No. Not since he was having a drink just after we came in."

Strangely enough, Greg and I ate without talking. But it wasn't an uncomfortable silence. The old feeling of just being happy together was re-establishing itself, and while it was nice — wonderful, in fact — I realized it was dangerous — for me. I shouldn't feel that way with a man I wasn't going to marry.

After a while Greg looked at me and smiled. "It's nice to be with you again, chicken," he said.

My heart gave a jump. If I said, "It's nice to be with you, too," would I be betraying Bryan? To be on the safe side, I just smiled and asked, "More chocolate cake?"

He said, "No, thanks," and put his empty tea cup on the silver tray resting on the low table before me.

"You really are the only girl in the world for me," he said, returning to his chair and lighting a cigarette.

I leaned over and placed my cup and saucer beside his. "What did you mean by 'before' on the card you sent with the roses?"

He grinned. "Before our separation, of course."

I felt myself blushing. "I wonder where Bryan is?" I said pointedly.

He shrugged. "Around somewhere."

I stood up. "I think I'll see if I can find him. *He* likes chocolate cake, too, even if he won't admit it."

Greg stood up politely, but let me go and stayed in the living room. I walked along the hall toward the kitchen. Just as I came to the back stairs leading up to Agnes's and John's quarters, I met Bryan coming down the stairs.

"What are you doing snooping around?" he asked crossly.

"I'm not snooping. I was looking for you. Don't you want some tea and chocolate cake?"

"No."

We stood looking at each other for a moment. It was silly, but I began to feel embarrassed. "Why were you up there?" I asked, suddenly feeling breathless.

"Any reason why I shouldn't be?" he snapped.

"No. But it's Agnes's and John's rooms."

"So?"

"So why would you be up there?"

He leaned against the wall, a tight look on his pale face, his blond hair looking dark in the hall shadows, his blue eyes darker than usual. "Agnes wanted me to get something for her."

Knowing Agnes would never ask Bryan to wait on her, I began to feel apprehensive. "Were you up there Friday morning?" I asked.

He stared at me. "What are you getting at?"

135

"I was almost hit on the head with an azalea plant. Remember?"

A peculiar look passed over his face; then he laughed, a little too loudly. "You don't think I threw the azalea pot at you, for gosh sakes!"

I backed away from him, but he reached for me and pulled me close to him. His arms went around me, and he began kissing me, more ardently than he ever had before.

I tried to respond, but I couldn't. So I just stood passively and submitted to his caresses until I heard Greg's voice say, "Pardon *me*," as he pushed past us to go out the door to the back garden. He banged the door as he went out, and I pulled away from Bryan. He laughed softly and went to the dining room for a drink. I had never known him to drink so much or so often as he had since we'd been at Shadow Acres this time. It worried me.

Chapter Twelve

I hadn't realized we would be questioned about the fire, but early that evening a man from the insurance company arrived and wanted to talk to me. I'd gone up to my room directly after dinner, which had been rather unpleasant because Bryan and Greg scarcely spoke to one another, and neither responded to my attempt to start a general and innocuous conversation.

Agnes had put the man in the living room where the fire was still comfortably blazing, probably because she had added a couple more logs. The man said his name was John Bellows and he would like to ask me a few questions. He was tall and thin and very white. He asked, "Were you asleep when the fire started, Miss Randall?"

I said, "Yes."

"Had you been smoking before you went to sleep?"

"No. I never smoke."

"But as I understand it, a partly smoked cigarette was found in your bed."

"Then someone else put it there."

"Have you any idea who?"

"No."

"Who was the last person you remember being in your room before you went to sleep?"

"Agnes, the housekeeper."

"Does she smoke?"

"I've never known her to."

"What kind of a cigarette was it?"

"I haven't the faintest idea."

"Had you locked your door before you went to bed?"

"No. I didn't even know there was a key to it."

"Did you lock your windows?"

"No. There was three of them. The housekeeper had opened the middle one before she left the room so I'd have fresh air while I was sleeping."

He gave me a long, searching look. "Have you any enemies here at Shadow Acres?"

I hesitated. "No. None that I know of."

"I understand a murder was committed here a few days ago."

"Either that or suicide."

"The police are inclined to think it was murder."

"That wasn't the decision at the inquest this afternoon."

"The police don't always show their hand right away."

I sat up straight now. "Why would you know more than the rest of us?" I demanded.

He smiled. "I'm an investigator, Miss Randall. It is my business to find out everything I can."

I was glad to see Greg appear at the doorway and said quickly, "Oh, Greg, this is Mr. Bellows from the fire insurance company. He is inquiring about the fire."

Greg came into the room and held out a hand to the inspector. "I'm Gregory Sedgwick," he said. "Can I help you?"

Mr. Bellows stood up and shook hands with him, saying, "Perhaps." Then they both sat down near me. "Tell me what you know about the fire," Mr. Bellows asked Greg.

Greg said, "Well, I'd been taking a walk around the grounds and was going upstairs to my room when I smelled smoke and saw it seeping out beneath the door where Reda — Miss Randall — was resting. I tried to open the door and called to her, but couldn't rouse her or get the door open. So I shouted for Bryan — my cousin, Bryan Sedgwick — and Agnes, the housekeeper. They both came running, and I ran downstairs and called the fire department, then got an extension ladder from the garage and climbed up to the windows I knew belonged to Miss Randall's room. She was at the center window by that time, and all the windows were locked. I called to her to turn the catch on the one where she was. She did, and I got it open and took her out — just in time. She passed out as I was carrying her down the ladder."

"Was the room on fire then?"

"To tell the truth, I didn't pay much attention. One side of the bed had small flames licking at it, and the rug between the bed and the door was ablaze, and the room was filled with smoke. But the only thing I was interested in was Miss Randall."

"Were her clothes on fire?" Mr. Bellows asked.

Greg grinned, and I felt my face getting warm. "What she had on was singed," he said, "and one of her hands and forearm had been burned."

"Then what?" Mr. Bellows asked.

"Well, I got her down on the back lawn just as the fire engine arrived, and behind it a police ambulance. They rushed her to the hospital."

"Are your hand and arm badly burned?" Mr. Bellows asked me.

I looked at Greg, and he said, "Not too badly. I talked to the doctor at the hospital about it, and he said it was only a first degree burn. It shouldn't leave any scars." He smiled over at me. "And it won't interfere with your playing the piano after it's healed," he told me.

Mr. Bellows wanted to question Agnes, John and Bryan, and then he wanted to see the room where the fire had been.

He left without giving us a clue to his deductions, and I'm sure we were all glad to see him go. He wasn't the type of person you'd choose to be shipwrecked with on a desert island.

The next morning, Tuesday, Bryan was arrested for the murder of his grandfather. No warning. Nothing.

About ten o'clock, two police cars arrived with two policemen in each car. We were dawdling over breakfast — Greg, Bryan and I. When the front doorbell rang, Agnes answered it, and almost instantly the four policemen were in the dining room. In just a couple of minutes more they were taking Bryan away.

I was so stunned I couldn't move. And Greg, though he jumped up and started to protest, was pushed aside roughly.

Naturally Bryan protested, but he didn't put up a fight. How could he, against four armed policemen?

After they'd gone, I said to Greg, "He didn't do it. I'm sure he didn't."

Greg, looking worried, said, "Maybe not. But now he will have to prove he didn't. Or his lawyer will."

"But can't we help him?"

"Only by being careful of what we say at the trial."

"But — then I can't tell the truth. I'll have to lie!"

"You mean about seeing him with the gun in his hand?"

"Yes."

"That would be just circumstantial evidence, anyway."

"But it might count against him."

Greg drew in a long breath and held it. "There is always the fact there was oil on a pair of gloves."

I stared at him. "What have you done with them?" I asked.

"I guess they are still in my pocket." He put his hand in his coat pocket and drew them out, smiling slightly. Then he tossed them across the table to me, and I was forced to catch them or they would have landed in my coffee cup. "Perhaps you'd better take charge of them. Keep them for evidence at the trial."

I quickly put them in my lap and covered them with my napkin. "You know I couldn't do that, any more than I could tell about Bryan coming out of the library that night with the gun in his hand."

Greg sat looking at me, a thoughtful expression on his rugged, handsome face. "Perhaps I'd better tell you," he said, "that the oil used on guns is different from the oil on those gloves."

I guess my eyes widened with surprise, but I couldn't speak, so he continued. "It just so happens that the oil on my gloves is 3-in-one oil, which I used to oil the windshield wipers on the car. They weren't working right, and the fog kept clouding the windshield."

I felt like a child receiving a deserved reprimand for a stupid action.

He got up from the table and walked to a window. With his back to me, he said, "If you want verification of that, give the gloves to the police and let them send them to the laboratory."

"I don't have to do that, Greg," I said. "I believe you."

"So what are you going to do with them?"

"I could put them back on the seat of your car, where I found them."

"You could."

After that there was silence in the huge room. I could hear Agnes clattering about

out in the kitchen. I'd have liked to go out for a walk, but decided against it. But the thought reminded me of the stone that had been thrown at me. I said, "Greg, that bluestone — could it have made a hole in my head if it had been thrown at me from a distance?"

He turned around to face me, his hands in his trouser pocket. "I doubt it," he said. "I've been thinking about it. It could have if it had been catapulted from a sling shot. Then it would have had enough force to hurt you."

"But it would have had to be a large sling shot. It's not exactly a pebble."

"That's right," he agreed. "Remember the big sling shot I had when we were kids? We used to catapult rotten apples at tree trunks with it, and rocks at imaginary foes, when we were sure no one was around to stop us."

"I remember," I said. "Do you know what ever happened to it?"

"No. It might be out in the garage. But I doubt it. It probably got thrown out after I went away to school."

I held his dark eyes with mine. "Suppose it didn't?"

"Then I — or someone else — could have used it to catapult the bluestone at you."

Chapter Thirteen

After Bryan's arrest, Greg and I were free to leave Shadow Acres. Mr. Sedgwick's funeral was to be the following day. We didn't know whether or not Bryan would be allowed to attend. Probably not.

I finally got around to phoning the music school and telling them I wouldn't be able to play at the recital. And I called the New York papers and asked them to put in an announcement to the effect that my wedding would have to be postponed indefinitely. Most people had read about the Shadow Acres tragedy and would not be surprised.

Later that day, Greg told me, "I've phoned Dad, and he and Mother are flying up for the funeral."

"Oh, I'm so glad!" I cried. "It will be nice to see them."

Greg said, "They will like seeing you, too. They were always very fond of you and hoped that some day you and I —"

He didn't finish but changed the subject abruptly. "Incidentally, Granddad's lawyer phoned and asked if Dad would be here. He doesn't want to read the will until Dad arrives."

"What about Bryan?" I couldn't help asking.

"If he is mentioned in the will, and he probably is, I — well, I don't know how that will be handled."

"Do you think your folks will be able to stay for Bryan's trial? Or come back for it?"

"I'm sure they will if they can. After all, he's their nephew. And he's going to need all the friends and relatives he can get. Not that there is anything they can do, at this point, except give him moral courage."

"Greg," I said, "you'll be on his side, won't you? You won't say anything against him?"

He looked at me thoughtfully. "Have I ever let him down?"

I shook my head. "No. Nor has he ever let you down. You've been like brothers."

"Yes, like brothers, only —"

"Only what?"

"Nothing. I was just thinking."

"You weren't on his side the night your grandfather died."

"No, I wasn't. It was all too much of a shock. But you needn't worry about me at the trial."

I said, "Greg, who was the girl you had in your room at college that time?"

146

He shrugged. "Just a girl."

"Was she pretty?"

"Very."

"And was she a girl of 'questionable character,' like they said?"

Greg gave me a twisted smile. "I don't believe so. It's not always the girl's fault. It always takes two to tango."

"Greg, why did you — ?"

He looked me straight in the eyes. "Chicken," he said, "that is a question you never ask a man."

My ready blush made my face and neck flame. We were lingering over our lunch in the dining room, and suddenly I had to get away — get away from Greg — from Shadow Acres — away from it all — now, before and forever, as Greg had written on his card.

I jumped up from the table. "I think I'll go home this afternoon," I announced.

"You mean down to the city?"

"Yes."

"But you can't drive with your bandaged arm and hand."

"I'll go by train. John will drive me to the station. There is a train every half-hour or so."

Getting up, Greg said, "I'll drive you down to the city."

147

At the dining room door, I turned. "No! I don't want you to. I want to go alone!"

"But you shouldn't," he protested. "There's your head — your hand and arm — the shocks you've had. You shouldn't go alone. You should be in bed right now."

He was right. I did feel weak and shaky. But I had to get away from him. "I'm all right," I lied. "Besides, I have to get some clothes. I can't go to the funeral tomorrow like this." I indicated Agnes's brown dress and my blue satin evening sandals that I was still wearing.

He came over and put an arm around me. "Give me your address and your keys, and I'll drive down and get whatever you need. Make me a list and tell me where to find things."

I was about to protest when I felt myself starting to sag.

As if from far away, I heard him call Agnes. And the next thing I knew, I was up in my room lying on the bed, and Agnes and Greg were standing beside me.

When I opened my eyes, Greg grinned. "Now will you give me that list?" he asked.

I nodded. "You won't need a list," I told him. "Just get me a few sets of underwear from the second long drawer of the dresser in the bedroom. Everything is piled in sets, according to color. Bring me a black and a couple of white sets. And in the closet you'll find a black wool dress. There is only one black wool. And bring me the green suit and the blouse hanging beside it. And a robe and slippers and the cosmetics that are on my dressing table."

"You're sure I won't need to make a list?" he asked, smiling.

"No, you have a good memory."

Our eyes met, and I wished I hadn't said that, so I hurried on, saying, "On the floor of the closet you'll find shoes. Bring me the black suedes and the green kids. In the top right-hand dresser drawer, you'll find matching gloves. And you'd better bring me a couple of hats. They're on the closet shelf. You'll be able to tell which go with which costume. Oh, and there's a black cloth coat with a mink collar. Bring that, too."

He grinned. "Okay. But suppose I get stopped for rifling your apartment?"

"I'll phone the doorman and tell him you're coming, and what you look like."

"*That* I'd like to hear," he teased.

I had to smile. "Oh, go along," I told him.

He said, "Okay. See you later."

It wasn't until I'd gotten the doorman on the phone and heard Greg drive away that I remembered I had his silver-framed photograph tucked away among my underwear. Bryan's had replaced his picture on my dresser.

Agnes insisted I rest for what remained of the afternoon, and I was only too glad to do so.

When I awoke, it was almost dark, and I felt much better. I was still fully dressed, still in Agnes's brown dress. As I was stretching with the all out abandon of a cat, there was a knock on my door. I called, "Who is it?" and reached for the bedside lamp, clicking it on.

Greg's voice said, "It's me. I have your things."

I got up and opened the door for him, snapping on lights as I went. "Your bags, miss," he said with a grin.

I had to laugh. He had a bag in each hand and two of my hats on his head, one on top of the other.

"You're a doll," I told him. "Thanks a million."

He came in, dropped the bags on the floor and put a hat on each of the posts at the foot of the bed. "I hope I've made the right selections," he said. "You didn't mention stockings, but I brought some anyway."

I wanted to hug him but refrained. "Thanks. I will need them."

"And I brought a couple of extra dresses, too. I hope you don't mind. There was plenty of room in the bags." He picked up one of the bags and put it on a bench that was at the foot of the bed, snapped it open and took out a teal blue velvet sheath with a white collar and cuffs. "I can't help feeling sentimental about this one," he said, holding it up. "You were wearing it on our last date. Remember?"

I almost snatched it from his hands. "Yes, I remember. I thought I'd thrown it out."

"As being contaminated?" His eyes questioned me.

I turned and walked to the closet and put the dress on a hanger. "Now you're being childish," I snapped.

He stood watching me as I unpacked the things he'd brought. The other dress was a beige lace, rather low-necked and sleeveless. I'd worn it to one of his frat dances his last year in college. "Why on earth did you bring this?" I asked as I hung it up.

"Because the night you wore it, we were very happy. You were very beautiful. And you told me you loved me very much."

I whirled around and faced him. "If you're trying to make me fall in love with you again, you are wasting your time!" I cried, not quite able to control my voice. "Because I won't. I love Bryan now and I always will, whether he is found guilty or not."

I snatched up some of the underwear to put in the dresser drawers, and his silver-framed photograph fell out. "Oh!" I cried. "I don't want *this*."

He smiled ruefully. "Then why have you kept it? And among your most intimate things?"

I snatched it up from the floor where it had fallen on a soft rug, which saved it from breaking. Then I threw it back into the bag. Greg watched me but said nothing.

When I finished unpacking the first bag, I closed it and put it in the closet, the picture still inside. Greg replaced it on the bench with the second bag. Then he said, "Well, I guess you'd rather I left you to finish in peace," and walked toward the door.

But I stopped him. "Thank you, Greg, for getting these things for me. I didn't mean to be so nasty. I'm just rather upset."

He smiled. "I understand," he said. "Think nothing of it. See you at dinner."

After he'd gone, I hurried through the rest of my unpacking; then I took a shower as best I could without getting my bandaged hand and arm wet, and put on fresh clothes. I topped the fresh, clean underwear with the teal blue dress, which, though I wouldn't admit it to Greg, I had kept for the very reason he'd mentioned. Only too well did I remember our last date. It had been during his spring vacation, and he was staying at his father's apartment in the city. I'd gone down to meet him for dinner and a movie. That was all there had been to it, but it had been a heavenly evening, as all our times together were.

When I joined him at the dinner table and he saw I was wearing the teal blue dress, he just smiled and looked happy, and my heart seemed to be melting and afraid. Afraid? Of what? Of discovering I was still in love with the cousin of the man I was going to marry?

Chapter Fourteen

The funeral for Mr. Sedgwick was private, held in a small Presbyterian church in the village. But although only the members of the family and a few very close friends were allowed inside the church, there were clusters of curious onlookers standing around outside.

Greg's mother and father had arrived late the previous evening and had stayed at the Inn in the village. I saw them for the first time when they came down the church aisle and joined me in the pew where I was sitting with Greg.

I was glad to see that neither Natalie nor Gregory had changed much since I'd last seen them. Natalie was still beautiful and her husband still handsome, although he had put on a little weight and had a few gray hairs at his temples.

We smiled at each other, and I moved over to make room for them beside their son.

Bryan didn't come to the funeral, either from choice or because he wasn't allowed to. I suppose if he had he would have been sent with a police escort, and he wouldn't have wanted to come that way.

Agnes and John were there, as well as a few of the people from Mr. Sedgwick's office in the city and a few of the local people who had been his friends through the years.

There were many flowers, and their sweetness made me somewhat faint. I was glad when it was all over and I could get out into the cold, fresh air.

The cemetery was within the limits of the village, and that part of it was soon over.

When we reached Shadow Acres — Greg, his mother and father, John and Agnes — Agnes said she would have lunch ready in a jiffy.

During lunch, Greg's mother and father and I got reacquainted. They wanted to know all about what I had done since the death of my parents. Neither of them had been to either my mother's or father's funeral. I told them my mother had died of cancer three years ago, and afterwards Dad and I had stayed in the house with a housekeeper until my father had had a heart attack about a year ago. Then I'd moved into the city to continue my study of music. I'd been left fairly well off, as far as money was concerned, so I hadn't had to get a job.

I noticed they avoided touching on the reason for my breakup with their son and my subsequent engagement to Bryan, although I surmised they knew about it.

The lawyer came in the afternoon, and when he read the will there were some surprises. John and Agnes had been left a modest life income. Bryan, who was then twenty-two, had been left fifty thousand dollars, provided he didn't marry until he was twenty-five. If he did, his share was to go to his cousin, Greg. Greg had been left fifty thousand unconditionally. And Greg's father had been left the residue of the estate, which included Shadow Acres. In all, nearly a million.

When the lawyer had finished reading the will, no one spoke for a long time. Then Greg's father said, "Bless him, he always tried to be fair."

Agnes said, "He was a fine man, and John and I are very grateful. Aren't we, John?"

John, his white face looking as if it were carved out of stone, just grunted.

Then everyone looked at me, and I spoke my thoughts. "I don't understand why he didn't want Bryan to marry until he was twenty-five. He knew we were being married next week."

The lawyer cleared his throat. He was tall and thin and a sort of sand color — hair, eyes, face and suit. And his name was Mr. Sanders. "This will was made five years ago, just after his wife died," he told me. "He seemed to have the feeling that Bryan was unstable in some ways and might make the mistake of marrying the wrong girl. He felt if he waited until he was twenty-five, he'd be more apt to choose wisely."

"But he seemed pleased about Bryan marrying me."

The lawyer nodded. "He was — very pleased. I might as well tell you he'd intended changing his will accordingly."

"Then why do you suppose he summoned Bryan and me to come up here that night? To tell us that?"

The lawyer shrugged. "Perhaps to tell you, and to give you his blessing."

"No. He sounded too upset for anything like that."

"Perhaps he was going to ask you to wait until Bryan was twenty-five."

"No, I don't believe that, either. We've been engaged for six months, and he seemed happy about it."

Mr. Sanders began to gather together his papers and put them into his brief case. "Mr. Sedgwick had a very strong family pride," he said. "And he has always worried about his grandson, Bryan."

"But why Bryan?" I asked. "He has always been the epitome of everything good." I noticed Greg exchange glances with his mother and father.

Mr. Sanders looked at me over the tops of his glasses. "Is that why he is in prison now?" he asked.

I felt as if I'd been struck a heavy blow. For a moment I couldn't speak. When I could, I said, "That is a strange thing to say!"

He didn't answer me, nor did anyone else speak. For a moment I felt as if everyone in the room were against me — and Bryan. I got up and ran from the room and out to the frozen back garden. It was cold, but my black wool dress was warm.

I would have liked to go into the woods but dared not. After a while, Agnes came out to me with the heavy sweater of Mr. Sedgwick's I'd worn that other day. It smelled fresh and clean. She'd probably washed it when she'd washed my things. She said, "You'll catch your death. Besides, he's gone. You can come in any time now. I'm going to fix tea."

"I don't want any," I said, almost sniffling, because the cold wind was making my nose run.

"Suit yourself," she said, and returned to the house.

Seeing me wandering around the frozen garden, anyone would have deduced that I'd come out to think. But I wasn't thinking. I was too numb. Things had gone too far. And yet there was still further to go. On and on — up to and through the trial of Bryan for the murder of his grandfather. And even further. But how could I think of that? If Bryan was convicted, what would be left for me?

After a while, Agnes opened the back door and called, "Tea's ready!"

I didn't answer her, but I decided I might as well go inside. I'd have to face them all again eventually.

When I went in, they were all in the living room. That is, Greg and his mother and father were. Natalie was sitting behind the low table, pouring the tea. She looked lovely in a simple black silk dress, her titian hair piled on top of her head in puffs. When she saw me come in, she smiled and asked, "Strong or weak, Reda?"

I said, "Strong, please. And plain. Just a piece of lemon."

Greg and his father had risen to their feet at my entrance. Now Greg took my arm and led me to a settee, sitting down beside me, and his father brought me my tea.

Suddenly I wanted to cry. I shouldn't hold anything against those three people. They were so very kind, so very dear to me. Perhaps I should let bygones be bygones and forgive Greg. That was what he had said he would have counted on, if he'd stayed instead of running away. He'd admitted it himself.

He got up and took a plate of cup cakes from the silver tray and passed them. Agnes must have made them early that morning. I shook my head. I couldn't possibly eat anything. I just hoped the tea would slide down easily.

After she'd served everybody, Natalie leaned back and sipped her own tea. "Now then," she said, "let's talk this thing out — the four of us." She made it sound as if we four belonged together, and my heart began to get a nice warm feeling.

Greg said, "I don't think Reda is quite up to hearing the truth, Mother."

"I think she can stand it," his mother said. She turned to me. "You see, dear, Bryan isn't and never has been the paragon of virtue you've always thought him to be."

Greg said, "Mother, *please!*"

But his mother shook her head at him. "Nor has Greg ever been the hellion he's let people believe him to be," she told me.

Greg made a quick movement and spilled some of his tea, wiping it up with his napkin.

"Mother, stop it!" he said. "It won't do any good. It's too late."

"It's never too late, son," his father said. "We all make mistakes. Your mother and I made a very serious one when we let the family interfere in our life. But thank heaven we are together again now. Don't you and Reda make the same mistake."

I looked from one to the other. What could they mean? Natalie told me, "What you never knew, my dear," she said, "was that all the things Greg was accused of through the years were Bryan's misdeeds. But Greg always took the blame and covered up for him."

"And you and his father knew it — and let him?"

Natalie shook her head. "No, we didn't know for a long time. We, too, made the mistake of thinking Greg was the wild one."

I couldn't meet Greg's eyes, but in the sudden silence of the room I could hear him breathing heavily beside me on the settee. Then a log in the fireplace fell with a swhoosh and a sputtering of upward sparks.

"We didn't find out until the last time. Then we investigated and found out the truth. You see, we knew how much in love he was with you and couldn't believe he would betray you."

"You mean — ?"

"I mean the girl was Bryan's girl, not Greg's."

"But she was found in Greg's room!" I was almost screaming.

Natalie smiled. "Because Greg managed to get Bryan out on the fire-escape and take his place when he knew someone was coming."

"But it *was* Greg's room?"

"Oh, yes, it was Greg's room. Bryan was too clever to have the girl in his own room."

"Did Mr. Sedgwick know the truth?"

"Not at first. When he found out, he financed Greg's trip to South America. He said it would be good for him to get away and make a new life for himself — away from Bryan and the family. And although he never actually said so, we got the impression he had always been somewhat suspicious of Bryan's actions. And now his will has proved it."

I drew in my breath and let it out slowly. Then I turned to Greg. "Then it seems that I was the only one who believed the worst of you."

He patted my arm. "It was the natural thing for you to do."

"Was it?" I looked away, over to the fallen log, now slowly turning to a gray ash. Then I looked up and around at the other three in

162

the room. "Then you all believe Bryan is guilty of this last thing?"

"Not at all," Greg's father said. "A man is always innocent until he is proven guilty."

I looked at him. "But what chance has he got?" I cried. "You are all against him. Nobody is on his side but me."

"That's not true, chicken," Greg said quietly. "I love Bryan, like a brother. I always have. That is the reason I've always taken the blame for his escapades. So now that he is in real trouble, I'm not going to step aside and let him take the blame, if he didn't do it."

I twisted around on the settee so I was facing him. "But you can't take the blame for *this!* It's too serious."

He took the tea cup and saucer from my trembling hands and reached over and put it on the silver tray. Then he took my hand in his and looked down into my troubled eyes. "Look, chicken," he said, "let me worry about this. And you stop worrying about Bryan."

Tears began to run down my cheeks, and I couldn't speak. Natalie and Greg's father put their cups and saucers on the tray. Then Natalie said, "My dear, I've learned from experiences that men by the name of Gregory Sedgwick are good men to put your faith in."

I began to cry for real then, and covered my face with my unbandaged hand. Natalie and Greg's father got up and quickly left the room, and Greg sat beside me and let me cry. When I had no more tears left, he dried my eyes and face with his handkerchief. "Now," he said, "suppose you and I have a little talk."

I sighed. "Oh, not now. Please, Greg!"

He took my upper arms in his strong hands. "Yes, *now!*" he said, giving me a little shake. "To begin with, I don't think Bryan is guilty. And I think I can prove it. At least I am going to try."

I stared at him. "But if he didn't do it, who did? There was no one around but us three."

"No one we saw. That doesn't mean no one was there — somewhere — or had been."

"But who? Have you any idea?"

He nodded. "Yes. I have a very definite idea."

"But who?"

"If I told you, you'd be in danger. You've had enough near-accidents."

"But if you know, then *you* are in danger!"

"I'll be on the lookout."

"But, Greg," I cried, "nothing must happen to *you*. I couldn't bear it!"

He took me in his arms and kissed me tenderly. "And nothing must happen to *you*, chicken," he said. "I couldn't bear *that*." His lips claimed mine, and for the first time since I'd come to Shadow Acres, that fatal Thursday night, I felt safe.

Agnes's voice brought me back to reality by asking, "Shall I take the tea things?"

Greg stopped kissing me, but he kept his arms around me as he said, "Yes, Agnes. We've finished."

She picked up the laden silver tray. "Are your mother and father staying the night here?" she asked him.

"I don't know. We'll have to ask them."

"They're over in the library," she told us. Then, stopping in the doorway, she said, "And if I may say so, Miss Reda, you're now exactly where you belong." With that cryptic remark, she stalked out, the tea things clinking on the silver tray as she walked down the hall to the kitchen.

Chapter Fifteen

Natalie and Gregory Sedgwick decided to stay at Shadow Acres and drove down to the Inn for their things. And it was a lucky thing Greg and I weren't left alone that night, because in the middle of the night I awakened with the most horrible feeling I'd ever had. I couldn't breathe because something was over my face. I tried to discover what, but couldn't. All I could tell was that it was awfully dark and I was smothering. I began to fight desperately, as well as I could with one hand and arm bandaged, and after struggling for what seemed like an eternity I managed to squirm away from whatever it was that was covering my face. Flinging the thing away from me with my good arm, I rolled to the other side of the bed and, with what breath I had left, began to scream.

I was afraid to look to see who was in the room, but I could feel a presence — an evil, menacing one. And did I imagine it, or was there a faint scent of gardenia?

I dropped to the floor on my good hand and knees, crouching almost under the bed, and kept screaming at the top of my voice.

I didn't hear any footsteps, but I did hear the door closing. Still I stayed where I was. Then the door opened, and Natalie and Gregory rushed in and snapped on the overhead light.

"Reda!" they cried in unison. "Where are you? What's the matter?"

I managed to get up on the bed and, gasping for breath, now it was all over, I said, "Somebody was trying to smother me!"

The bed was a double bed and had two pillows. But I used only one. The other was in the middle of the floor where it must have landed when I'd made my final successful struggle to free myself.

Gregory stooped and picked it up and tossed it on the bed. "You must have been having a nightmare," he said.

"No!" I cried. "I woke up, and it was very real. Somebody was holding the pillow over my face!"

Natalie came and sat down on the bed beside me and put her arms around me. She had on an emerald green negligee, and her hair was hanging loose about her shoulders, and she looked beautiful. She smelt of *Muguet du Bois,* my favorite scent. "Poor child," she said. "No wonder you have nightmares, with the things that have been happening to you these last few days. Greg has told us all about it."

"But I tell you it wasn't a nightmare. It was real. Someone was here!"

"All right," Natalie said soothingly. "Do you want me to stay with you for the rest of the night?"

I said, "No, thanks. I guess I'll be all right. I'll lock my door this time. There's a key to this one." Then I asked, "Where is Greg?"

"In his room, sound asleep, I presume," his father said. "He's a heavy sleeper."

"Are you sure he is all right?" I asked anxiously.

He looked surprised at my question. "You certainly don't think *he* tried to smother you, do you?"

"No. No, I don't. But he may be in danger, too. Oh, don't you understand? There is someone here who wants to kill me. And maybe Greg too!"

"But there is no one in the house except us and Agnes and John. And certainly *they* wouldn't want to hurt you, either of you."

I reached for my robe and found my slippers that had been kicked under the bed. "Please!" I pleaded. "Let's go to Greg's room. I want to be sure he is all right."

His father shrugged, and Natalie said,

"Why not? His room is just across the hall."

Gregory reached his son's door first and opened it quietly. The room was dark — ominously still. There was no sound of a sleeping man breathing.

"Greg?" Natalie said.

There was no answer.

The light switch was beside the door, and I clicked it on. But Greg wasn't there. His bed was open and had been slept in, or at least laid on, but he was no longer in it. And his robe and slippers were gone.

Then I saw the slingshot. It was on the dresser — and it was the giant one, the one that would have been large enough to catapult the piece of bluestone at my head! And the bluestone was laying beside it!

"That's strange," Gregory said. "Where can he be?"

"Perhaps in the bathroom?" his mother suggested, going over to the room which opened off the bedroom. He wasn't there.

"Maybe downstairs getting something to eat?" his father said. "He does that sometimes when he can't sleep."

We all went downstairs, turning on lights as we went. But he wasn't there. With each empty room, my heart sank lower and lower. Where could he be? Was he hurt? Dead?

At the foot of the stairs to Agnes's and

John's quarters, I stopped and looked up. It was dark up there, and there was no sound. I suggested, "Maybe we should get Agnes and John." But Gregory said, "Oh, don't bother them. There is probably some simple explanation."

I walked to the back door in the hall and looked out. It was beginning to get foggy, and I could feel the damp cold seeping in around the door frame. Then I saw, or thought I saw, a light moving in the garage. But with the fog, it was hard to tell. Could it be Greg? But why would he be out there at this time of night? Just then the grandfather clock in the hall struck three with an eerie whirring sound. It made me jump.

Natalie said, "As long as we're down here, why don't we have some hot tea?"

"Sounds good," I said. "I'll put on some water."

Natalie went to the refrigerator and began assembling things for sandwiches.

It was cold, and Gregory went into the hall to turn up the thermostat. In a couple of minutes we heard a thud. Quickly Natalie and I looked at each other, both asking, "What was that?"

The sound seemed to come from the front of the hall, and Natalie called, "Gregory?"

I was nearest the door, so I looked out.

Then I cried, "It's Gregory! Quick!"

He was lying on the floor near the grandfather clock, and he was apparently unconscious. I ran to him, Natalie close behind me, and we both dropped to our knees beside him. He was on his face, and Natalie tried to turn him over, crying, "Gregory! Darling!"

I could feel goose flesh sprouting out all over me, but I couldn't speak. My voice seemed to have left me. But I managed to help Natalie turn the heavy man over so we could see his face. There didn't seem to be a mark on him, and there was no blood anywhere.

There wasn't much I could do with just one hand and arm, but I had the feeling that Natalie was glad I was there with her. I asked, "Could it be a heart attack?"

She shook her head. "No. His heart is fine."

"But then — what?"

My answer came from Bryan, who stepped out of the library, which was now dark, although I was sure we had snapped on the light by the door when we came downstairs. He had a gun in his hand, and it was pointed at me. "I hit him," he said.

"But why?" I managed to get to my feet and stand facing him.

"Because he got in my way. And if you get

in my way, I'll hit you, too. Or better still, I'll shoot you!"

"But I thought you were in prison." My voice worked, but not very well. I guess I'd screamed so hard upstairs I'd strained it.

He smiled rather sardonically. "I was. But I got out, thanks to Christine, who brought me clothes and hid them for me in a place where I could make a quick change."

"Christine?" I asked stupidly.

"Yes. Christine. You didn't know I knew her, did you?" He took a tighter grip on the gun.

"I didn't know she existed until a few days ago."

"That shows how stupid you are, my dear Reda."

Things began to fall into place in my confused mind, like small pieces of a jigsaw puzzle. "Was she the girl they found in Greg's room at college?"

He grinned. It gave him a strange expression. I'd never seen him grin before. He smiled and he laughed, but he never grinned. "The same," he said. "Surprised?"

"Well, yes, I am," I said, shivering from the chilliness of the hallway. Apparently Gregory hadn't quite made it to the thermostat before he was struck down.

Bryan began coming toward me, the black hole of the pistol pointing at my face. "Give me your ring," he said. "I'm going to need money."

Natalie was still on her knees beside her unconscious husband. She said very quietly, but in a voice that carried, "Put that gun down, Bryan. You've made enough trouble for Reda. Don't make any more."

He glanced down at her. "Hello, Aunt Natalie. Sorry I had to hurt Uncle Gregory, but — !"

She got to her feet. "You're desperate."

He nodded. "Yes, I am. I had to kill a guard to escape from prison, and I haven't any time to waste. They're probably after me now." He came closer to me and held out his left hand. "Come on; give me your ring. Quick! If you don't, I'll have to take it!"

I held out my left hand to him. My right hand was too heavily bandaged to be of use. Looking straight into his eyes, I said, "Take it. You put it on my finger; you can take it off."

He hesitated for a split-second; then, coming over to me, he began to work the ring from my finger. It wasn't easy, because his hand was trembling as much as mine.

Natalie stood watching us, her robe clutched around her. Her face was white, her green-gray eyes enormous. "You're a heel, Bryan, just like your father," she said in a ringing voice that seemed to fill the hall, right up to the top of the glass dome of the rotunda. At her feet her husband groaned. Quickly Bryan turned and pointed the gun at him.

"Don't you dare!" Natalie cried. "If you do, I'll tear you apart!"

Coming from the sweet, beautiful Natalie, it was almost funny. But of course nothing could have been funny under existing conditions.

Bryan looked at her, as surprised as I was; then he said, "You know I wouldn't, Aunt Natalie."

She heaved a heavy sigh. "You hit him!" she accused.

"I had to. He saw me and was going to grab me."

Just then a tall, blonde and very beautiful girl came down the back stairs. It could only be Christine. "Ready to go?" she asked Bryan. She had an overnight bag in her hand, and a cigarette was hanging from one side of her mouth.

"Almost," he said, backing away from me. He hadn't managed to get the ring from my finger. It was dangling over my knuckle. I went over to Christine and held out my hand. "You take it," I told her.

She looked surprised. "What?" she asked.

"The ring," Bryan told her. "Take it. We're going to need money."

She hesitated, but Bryan said, "Hurry up! We haven't any time to lose. They'll be after me."

I went closer to Christine and held my hand so she could take the ring. Her fingers were ice cold as they touched my hand. And she smelled of cheap toilet water. Gardenia.

Was she the one who had tried to smother me? Was she the one who had set my room on fire?

Gregory was beginning to move, and Natalie was on her knees beside him again.

I wondered where Greg was. Had it been he out in the garage with the light? I asked, "Where is Greg? Have you hurt him?"

Bryan had his left arm around Christine now; with his right hand he was pointing the gun at me again. Christine was putting my ring on her finger, and I noticed she already had on a wedding ring. "Not yet," he said. "But if he gets in my way, I will."

For a moment I stood there as if paralyzed, watching Bryan backing out of my life. But I couldn't let him go like that, with so many unanswered questions. So before he reached the door, I asked, "Bryan, did you kill your grandfather?"

He shook his head. "No. Christine did. It was an accident. She just wanted to scare him, and the gun went off."

"Did you know she'd killed him — that night?"

"No."

"When did you find out?"

"Not until today. I've thought all along it was Greg. But today she told me. She'd gone to the library to ask Granddad for money. And he refused. Said he wouldn't give her or me a nickel. They had an argument, and it happened — just before I got here."

"How did she get the gun?"

"Grandfather had been oiling it. It was lying on the desk."

I heard the girl draw in a quick breath, and her large blue eyes grew frightened. "I didn't mean it," she said shakily. "He'd found out about us — Bryan and me — and he was going to tell you. That's why he had you come up here that night. He was going to tell you and then have Bryan arrested."

"He'd found out about a check I'd forged his name to," Bryan said. "That's what really got him: the money. It was only for a thousand dollars, but that got him."

"But, Bryan, how could you?" I cried. "You've always been so honest, and the bank trusts you."

He smiled a twisted smile. "I'm honest all right. But it cost money to be engaged to you,

Reda. I figured I'd get it back after we were married, and then I'd repay Granddad."

I stared at him, then at Christine's left hand with the wedding ring on it — and now my engagement ring. "But what about her?" I asked him, nodding at Christine.

He shrugged. "We were married a few days before she was found in Greg's room up at college," he said.

"But then — how could you marry me?"

He shrugged again. "I thought I could get away with it. Nobody knew Christine and I were married, and I figured —" He hesitated, then went on, "You might as well know the truth. I thought after I married you, I could get some of your money and then go back to Christine."

I stared at him. His hand holding the gun had dropped to his side and was no longer a threat to me. "Then you never really loved me?"

"No. And you didn't love me, either."

Slowly and quietly the back door opened and Greg, in his bathrobe and slippers, stood there. Instantly taking in the situation, he just reached out and took the gun from Bryan's hand. He did it so quickly he caught Bryan unaware.

Bryan whirled around, but Greg had the gun pointed at him.

"Why, you — !" Bryan cried, lunging at him.

But Greg just gave him a shove toward the door. "Get out!" he told him. "You and Christine, too. Get out, and don't ever come back!"

Natalie was helping her husband to his feet, and Gregory was holding his hand to the back of his head.

Bryan and Christine were backing out the door, both looking scared to death.

"But, Greg," I cried. "You can't let them go. They are murderers, both of them."

Greg was pushing them out the door now, the gun poking into Bryan's ribs. "I know," Greg said, "but they won't get far." He pushed them out the door and closed it, and as we all stood there, listening, we heard a car motor being revved up in the driveway. Then, with a shower of gravel and squeaking wheels, the car zoomed down the driveway and out onto the road and away into the night.

When it was quiet again, Greg slipped the gun into a pocket of his bathrobe and went to help his mother with his father. They got him into the living room and onto a sofa. He assured us he was all right.

Feeling my knees begin to give way, I sank down on the nearest chair. "I wonder if Agnes and John knew?" I asked.

"I'd better go up and see if they are all right," Greg said, and hurried out of the room.

"But Christine wouldn't hurt her own parents!" I cried.

"That girl would do anything," Gregory said. "She's a bad egg."

In a few minutes Greg returned with Agnes and John in their bathrobes and slippers. Agnes was crying, and John, as usual, was stony-faced.

"They were tied up and gagged," Greg explained. He led Agnes to a chair and helped her into it. John stood stiff and straight in the doorway.

"Has Christine been here right along?" I asked Agnes.

She sniffed and nodded. "I tried to keep her out of sight," she sobbed.

"Then it was she I saw in the back garden that night?"

Agnes nodded, sobbing softly as if her heart were broken. "She didn't dare stay in the house that night with the police around."

"And it was she who pushed the azalea plant off the roof?"

Agnes nodded again.

"And set fire to my room?"

Agnes looked up at me imploringly. "Oh, yes! Yes!" she almost screamed. "She did it all! And she took my bunch of keys and found a key to lock your door. And she made Bryan what he turned into!"

Gregory sat up then, holding onto his head. "Not entirely," he said. "Bryan had a good start — from birth."

I turned to Greg. "Were you out in the garage a little while ago?"

"Yes. I was looking for the slingshot."

"It's up on the dresser in your room," I told him.

"But how did it get there?"

"Didn't you put it there?"

"No. And it wasn't there when I went to bed. I took the bluestone out of my pocket and put it on the dresser, but I didn't know where the slingshot was."

John took a step into the room. His bony hands were clenched at his sides. "It was up in our room," he said. "Christine took it after she and Bryan tied us up."

I couldn't help but feel sorry for him. "John," I said, "was it you who hit me with the bluestone?"

He nodded, his face completely without expression. "Yes, Miss Reda. I'm sorry."

"But why, John?" I felt as if I were going to faint but fought it, breathing deeply and gritting my teeth.

John looked down at the floor. He

couldn't meet my eyes. "Because you stood in the way of my daughter's happiness," he said huskily. "She loved Bryan, and he was her husband and had been for two years. You had no right to marry him!"

"But I didn't know," I protested. "Have you known right along?"

Agnes answered for him. "No. We didn't know until last week. Then she came up to us and told us she was pregnant and — and —" She began to sob again.

"Did you know she was the one — up at college?"

She nodded. "Yes. She'd gotten herself a job in a restaurant in New Haven so she could get acquainted with him."

"Then he never knew her around the house here?"

"No. I told you. I kept her away from the house. But she always wanted something better than she had. And she decided she was going to get one of the Sedgwick boys."

I glanced at Greg. "And she decided on Bryan?"

Agnes gulped. "She tried young Mr. Greg first. But he was in love with you and wouldn't have anything to do with her or any other girl."

My eyes filled with quick tears, and I

181

could feel a sob rising from deep within me, but I choked it back.

Just then the phone rang, and we all jumped. After a moment, as it kept ringing, Greg went into the hall and answered it. As we all listened, he said, "Oh! Yes, this is Shadow Acres. Yes, he's my cousin. The girl? She was his wife. Yes, I'll come right down."

He returned to the room and looked from one to the other of us. Then to Agnes and John he said, "I'm sorry. They had an accident. Hit that big tree at the turn in the road."

Agnes looked at him mutely. John asked, "Are they — ?"

"Both killed instantly," Greg said reluctantly.

Agnes let out a shriek. John went to her and put his arms around her, and she hid her face against his robe. Greg went over and patted Agnes's shoulder. "Better this way," he said gently, "than the police picking them up and then their having to stand trial and being convicted for murder, as they surely would have been."

But it isn't easy to be reconciled to a great loss by a logical rationalization of the whys and wherefores, and Agnes just cried harder.

Gregory and Natalie reached for each

182

other's hands, their eyes filling with tears.

For a moment my eyes met Greg's; then I was in his arms and he was holding me close. I was shaking from head to foot, but I couldn't cry. My eyes were wet, but the tears stayed in them.

Finally Greg said, "I'd better go. They want me to identify them."

John's voice, sounding like a foghorn, said, "I'll go with you."

Gregory asked, "Want me to go with you, son?" But Greg said, "No, you stay with the girls." He included Agnes in his glance, and she cried harder than ever.

Chapter Sixteen

For the next few days Natalie and I took over the housekeeping. Agnes was kept under sedation by the doctor. John stayed with her as much as he could, but sometimes he just had to get out of the house and go for long walks in the woods.

Greg took care of the reporters and the police had protected his mother and me from their questioning and prying as much as they could.

Of course the whole tragic story had to be told, and the newspapers made as much of it as they could for nearly a week. Then other more important things happening in the world pushed our story off the front pages and into limbo, where it belonged.

Christine and Bryan were given a double funeral in the same church where Mr. Sedgwick's had been held, and Christine was buried beside Bryan in the Sedgwick plot, as one of the family. As I look back on it, I think Bryan loved Christine as much as he was capable of loving anyone but himself.

It was all very sad, and Agnes had to be

given tranquillizers the day of the funeral in order to attend. We insisted she and John sit with us in the family pew, and she went through the service in the church and the short burial service at the cemetery like a sleepwalker.

John begged my forgiveness for having catapulated the bluestone at me, and in the final days of our stay at Shadow Acres became quite human and less stony-faced.

The night of the final tragedy I had wanted to ask Greg if he had known who Christine was at the time of the affair at college, but things happened too fast. However, the day it all came out in the papers, Greg took me for a walk in the woods early in the morning and explained the whole thing to me.

As Agnes had told me, Christine had gone up to New Haven and gotten herself a job in a restaurant that was patronized by the college boys. She was a beautiful girl with a luscious figure, and was soon a favorite with the patrons of the restaurant.

Whenever Greg was there, she went out of her way to get him to notice her. And he did. But he never asked her for a date. On the other hand, Bryan did, and soon they were dating frequently. Greg had warned Bryan to watch his step, but it was no use. Then he began bringing her to the frat house where they lived.

Up to that time Greg hadn't known who she was, nor had Bryan, not even when he married her. She gave her right name but it didn't mean anything to them, as they never thought of the servants at Shadow Acres as anything more than Agnes and John. As a matter of fact, if they'd ever heard their last name, they'd forgotten it.

Even when Greg's parents had investigated the reason for their son being expelled from college, they hadn't found out the girl's connection with Agnes and John. Nor did anyone know Bryan had married her until Mr. Sedgwick made his private investigation into Bryan's affairs. With the help of the lawyer, Mr. Sanders, he even went so far as to have him trailed, which was what eventually led to his association with Christine. Then it was discovered that Bryan used to go to her apartment after leaving me in the evenings, often spending the night there.

When Mr. Sedgwick finally found out Bryan had married her two years ago in a small town in Connecticut, he was furious. That was why he had called me that fatal night. Naturally, he couldn't let me go through with my wedding to Bryan.

He had also called Bryan and Christine

and told them to be there at the same time, choosing a Thursday night when he knew Agnes and John would be out. Up to that time he hadn't let Christine's parents know what he had found out. He had probably figured they must have known about their daughter's marriage and had kept it secret from him for the same reason Bryan had — because they hoped Bryan would inherit Shadow Acres eventually but were afraid he wouldn't if he married against his grandfather's wishes.

But as it turned out, even Agnes and John didn't know Christine and Bryan were married until Christine told them she was pregnant. They had known she was the girl up at college, but had kept that to themselves for fear of losing their jobs.

As Greg told me what he knew of the story and I told him what Agnes had told me, we were strolling through the frozen woods, hand in hand. It was like old times, in spite of our unpleasant conversation. "But you said you thought you knew who had killed your grandfather," I reminded him.

"I did. I thought it was John, after I got over thinking it was Bryan."

"But why John?"

"Well, I thought he acted strange that night when he and Agnes came in and the police questioned him. And when you were hit with the bluestone, I began to realize John would have been the only one to know where my rock collection was kept. And John would have known where the slingshot was, if it was still around, out in the garage. And it was John who had cleaned up the broken azalea plant before anyone else discovered it."

"But you didn't know Christine was here?"

"No. How could I? I did have some suspicions of Agnes, as well as John, but I couldn't understand why they would have anything against you."

I sighed. "Poor Agnes and John. They did what they thought was best for their daughter — and it all went wrong."

"Yes. It would have been better for the girl if she'd been allowed to grow up here at Shadow Acres."

"Then Mr. Sanders knew what it was all about the day he read the will?"

"He knew about Bryan and Christine being married, yes."

"But why did he pretend not to know why Mr. Sedgwick had summoned Bryan and me that night?"

"I guessed at that point he decided it wasn't any use. If Bryan had been brought to trial, it would have come out then."

"I still think he should have told us."

"I do, too, but sometimes it's hard to know why lawyers do things."

We were in a dense part of the woods by that time, and when we stopped talking there was no sound but an occasional bird, or the crackling of a twig, strained too much by the cold. A pale sun filtered through the bare branches of the trees, lighting our faces and bringing a promise of a bright, though still distant spring.

Suddenly Greg stopped walking and pulled me around so we were face to face. His dark eyes, sparkling from a stray sunbeam, looked deeply into mine. "Chicken," he said, "you're mine again."

I caught my breath. "I've always been yours, Greg, even when I was trying to deny it to myself and everyone else."

His arms went around me and held me close to him. "I'm going back to Brazil the end of the week," he said. "Come with me?"

Our lips were only about an inch apart, and I was leaning heavily against him. "You still want me?" I whispered.

"Want you, chicken?" he said. "I've never stopped wanting you. But if you don't want to marry me right away, I can wait. Mother and Dad will be going back with me. They think they'll stay down there for a while. Dad wants to take time out to write a book, and Mother is interested in the little theater movement down there. So you can stay with them until you feel you want to come to me." His lips were gently touching mine now, and I was standing on tiptoe to make it easier for him.

"I don't want to wait at all," I told him honestly. "But I suppose I should let my hand and arm heal first. And I'll have to give up my apartment and do something with my furniture. And I'll have to let them know at the music school that I won't be coming back."

He smiled and held me even closer. "They have music and musicians down in Brazil, too," he said. "And I'll have a concert grand sent out to the ranch for you."

"You won't mind my keeping on with my music?"

"Of course not, chicken. It's part of you. And I want every bit of you — for always." Then he kissed me, and it seemed as if the sun became brighter and all the birds in the woods began to sing at once. Or maybe it was angels singing. Or the woods could have been heaven. How was a girl to know?

Well, Greg, his mother and father and I

will be in Brazil for Christmas, and it will be summertime and flowers will be blooming. Greg and I are going to be married on Valentine's Day. And I'm the happiest girl in the world.

Agnes and John are retiring to Florida, and Shadow Acres is being sold to a boys' school.

And so, as I look back upon it all, I realize it was foolish of me to think I was responsible for any of it. And I am glad I was born into the Randall family, who were so closely associated with the Sedgwick family. Otherwise, how would I ever have found Greg in this great big world so full of people?

We hope you have enjoyed this Large Print book. Other Thorndike Press or Chivers Press Large Print books are available at your library or directly from the publishers.

For more information about current and upcoming titles, please call or write, without obligation, to:

Thorndike Press
P.O. Box 159
Thorndike, Maine 04986 USA
Tel. (800) 223-1244
Tel. (800) 223-6121
OR

Chivers Press Limited
Windsor Bridge Road
Bath BA2 3AX
England
Tel. (0225) 335336

All our Large Print titles are designed for easy reading, and all our books are made to last.